SHOOT OUT AT
HELLYER'S CREEK

Paid to mind other folks' business, Joshua Dillard did it with a .45 Colt Peacemaker. But he also had a mission of his own and when Butch Simich and his bunch stuck up the stage from Tucson he swung into vengeful action. The fight led into treacherous territory, up against rogue town marshal Virgil Lyons and saloonkeeper Dice Sanders, whose greed for women and money produced mayhem – and the most violent gun battle one-horse Hellyer's Creek had ever seen.

SHOOTOUT AT HELLYER'S CREEK

Shootout At Hellyer's Creek

by

Chap O'Keefe

Dales Large Print Books
Long Preston, North Yorkshire,
BD23 4ND, England.

British Library Cataloguing in Publication Data.   ●
_____

O'Keefe, Chap
    Shootout at Hellyer's Creek.

    A catalogue record of this book is
    available from the British Library

    ISBN   978-1-84262-787-7 pbk

First published in Great Britain in 1994 by Robert Hale Limited

Published in Large Print 2010 by arrangement with
Keith Chapman

Dales Large Print is an imprint of Library Magna Books Ltd.

Printed and bound in Great Britain by
T.J. (International) Ltd., Cornwall, PL28 8RW

1

Stage Stickup

'Whip' O'Reilly sent the long lash snaking above the heads of his four-in-hand with a heat-splitting crack. The vicious sound bounced and echoed off the towering, weather-etched boulders flanking the stage road where it wound its path tortuously to ascend the steepness of the mountainside.

The stench of horse sweat was pungent in the stifling stillness; the team's laboured breathing and the creak of harness and coach thoroughbraces of thickest steer hide loud in the baking silence.

'Giddap thar!' O'Reilly croaked.

He deftly manipulated the lines in his gnarled hands. Fine adjustments of the rein lengths, combined with canny use of whip and footbrake gave the oldster superb, independent control of each of the four horses and the heavily-laden stagecoach.

The man who sat alongside him high on the box marvelled at Whip's sensitive reinsmanship. On the westbound run from Tucson to Hellyer's Creek, O'Reilly was the ablest and most experienced, they'd told him. And now he could believe it. He'd needed the best, because he was a special courier for Wells, Fargo & Company, the big banking and freighting enterprise, and in his charge was fifty thousand dollars in United States bills and coin.

The bank messenger, though a taciturn man and large and capable in a land where that was somehow the expected norm, likewise took silent reassurance from the presence of the other fellow who rode on the outside of the stage. This was a shotgun guard who sat atop at the rear, eyes peeled in the harsh glare that beat down from a white-hot ball of fire in a sky of intense blue.

Of course, there was going to be no trouble.

'Them thar hills 'ud be full o' scoundrels o' every stripe – it's home to the fiddle-foots an' the grub-liners an' a reg'lar stampin' ground for the owlhoots,' O'Reilly had opined in Tucson, screwing up his wind- and sun-ravaged face in a heavy frown. 'Hombres thet ain't trusted by their own mothers!' He spat his chaw into the dust.

'But none of them know about this consignment,' the impassive-faced Wells Fargo man told the whiskered oldster. 'The bank's security is very tight. Only one man in this territory has any prior notice of it – the manager of the recipient bank in Hellyer's Creek. And the money will be in his vault before the word can be gotten out.'

'Then I kin git yuh to Hellyer's Creek shore 'nuff,' Whip acknowledged. 'Ain't I done the run a million times afore?'

'The stage line has every confidence in you,' said the Wells Fargo representative.

The close-mouthed man chose not to travel inside, where two passengers occupied the seats for nine, but bestowed on himself the privilege of riding with the driver on his lofty perch. From the little bits of information Whip managed to dredge out of him, he learned that Wells Fargo was expanding its banking operations as a hedge against losses on its Pony Express undertaking and in freighting competition with the ever-extending railroads.

Part of the strategy was investing in co-operative ventures with small local banks. Like it had done in other places, Wells Fargo was speculating on an expansion of ranching and mining operations around the township of Hellyer's Creek. The ready cash would stimulate activity in the town and its environs in the form of loans.

So now the stage climbed into the mountains and all was seemingly well, except for the discomforts of the heat and the jolting roughness of the trail.

Inside the coach, Clement P. Conway took off his grey derby, fanned his flushed cheeks with it and mopped his brow with a large Irish linen handkerchief. He was unaccustomed to the rigours of such travel, but accepted them stoically. They were, he suspected, but a small and initial part of the price he had to pay in his earnest desire to venture West, beyond the end of the rails.

'Of course,' chattered his companion passenger, 'it can be much, much worse, darling.'

Inwardly Clem groaned. Would this woman never hold her peace? She'd subjected him to a constant, garrulous barrage since they'd pulled out of the depot in Tucson, alongside the main district offices of Wells Fargo.

'Yes,' she gushed on. 'You should try the night mail in winter with a sleety blizzard driving in on you, and when the ruts are full of slushy mud and the coach slips and slides and bogs down...'

The nauseous feeling in Clem's stomach freshly swelled. 'I'd prefer not to,' he said, clenching his teeth.

The woman flashed him a self-deprecating smile. 'Of course, it's only a very short while back I was a young tenderfoot myself, darling, fresh to the ways of the frontier. I do surely sympathise.'

The coyness seemed out-of-place with her and grated.

Clem adjusted his steel-rimmed spectacles. He found her claim to recent youth and freshness doubtful. Lucia Marques had already regaled him with the highlights of her life – several times over, it seemed – and though her face was carefully masked with artful use of powder and paint, maturity and experience had also left their mark. In fact, he thought it likely youth had deleted itself from the Marques catalogue of assets even before she'd come to the New World.

Lucia (though she didn't tell Clem all of this) had been born plain Lucy Murgatroyd in Liverpool, England, better than thirty years ago. Orphaned at seven, she'd lived by her wits in the back streets and along the docks. She'd run errands, done odd jobs, worked as a housemaid. Then at sixteen, and blooming quite remarkably, she'd been engaged by a travelling theatrical company on the strength of an audition of sorts with the lecherous manager and lead performer.

Arriving in Portsmouth, and maybe recognising her thespian limitations, she eloped with a dashing young English Army officer. The liaison lasted barely long enough to carry her across the Channel to marriage and the Continent, where a year later she became the mistress of a darkly handsome Castilian nobleman, who (alas!) was shot dead – murdered – by brigands in the pay of his wife and political enemies.

She then toured Spain, Bavaria, Italy and Greece, living on her beauty and her wiles, sometime actress, sometime paramour. A second marriage, to a wealthy Neapolitan merchant, proved as unsatisfying as her first, and she sailed for America with another theatrical troupe.

Three years ago found her as a solo attraction on the stage in San Francisco, where she was pelted with spoilt eggs by an unappreciative populace quickly tired of the exposure of her fleshly allures. Her career on the boards was truly on the slide, her youthful bloom spent. She thankfully hitched up a third time with a well-heeled professional gambling man, one Daniel 'Dice' Sanders.

Was it third time lucky?

Clem got the impression that Lucia thought the luck had been all on the side of her tinhorn husband. Accused of being a card shark by men who didn't mess around, Dice Sanders had fled to the backwater of Hellyer's Creek.

The furthest reaches of Arizona in the eighteen-eighties, though no place for the faint-hearted, the squeamish or the weak, were somewhere a man might lie low awhiles while the dust settled down his back-trail. And Sanders had clearly prospered in his new milieu.

'Dice set up the Silver Buckle Saloon. You might call it the social hub of the town,' Lucia said. A hint of pride in her position crept into her voice. Maybe she'd come to accept her lot as a big fish in a small pond,

Clem thought. In recounting her tempestuous past, he'd sensed regrets for the present amidst the lusty nostalgia.

But certainly Lucia displayed material wealth. The purpose of her excursion to Tucson had apparently been solely pleasure. Her bonnet and travelling cape looked expensive and her ruffled skirt seemed as wide as the stage itself, taking up space that might rightly have been other passengers'.

She'd also been more than passingly interested in the stage's special cargo. Her own leather trunk, heavy with the gewgaws and fripperies she'd purchased in the emporiums of Tucson, had been relegated to a roping-down on the roof of the coach. Into the locked compartment under the driver's seat had gone sack after bulging canvas sack stencilled 'WELLS FARGO'. More of them had been loaded under the unoccupied seats in the passenger compartment. Several strongboxes had gone onto the platform at the rear and been enclosed in black oiled leather to form a boot.

'All this cash in circulation in Hellyer's Creek!' Lucia trilled. 'A flow of money is just what bank and town needs. It will show folks the powers-that-be have confidence in our little community's future and stability. Isn't it exciting, Mr Conway?' She couldn't have shown much more enthusiasm had the *dinero* been destined for her own personal purse.

Indeed, a proportion of it might well be, Clem now reflected, thoroughly apprised of her station in life as Mrs Daniel Sanders, wife to the proprietor of the town's brightest watering hole and gambling resort.

With her description of herself as a recent tenderfoot, Lucia finally seemed to tire of self-aggrandisement. She was in the company of a strange and personable *man* heading for what was now, like it or not, her home town. Curiosity, and other earthier things, compelled her interest.

She sensed a mystery.

Clem fanned himself again with his hat, and she tried unashamedly to read the label on the sweatband. 'New York City,' she picked out. 'I realised you were an Easterner, darling, but is that where you hail from?'

'Why, yes,' Clem answered cautiously. He pressed his pinstripe-suited shoulders into the leather of the seat cushions, bracing himself against the sway of the coach.

The woman's black-lashed eyes roamed to the rack over his head where he'd slung his portmanteau, a piece of baggage that stamped him, along with his neat store clothes, as a stranger to this range. He was just as obviously not the usual home-seeking immigrant.

'And what line of business takes you to Hellyer's Creek?' she asked boldly.

'You could call me a – a scribe,' Clem prevaricated. He felt doubly uncomfortable.

'A *what?*' If he'd thought this would fox Lucia, he was mistaken. 'Do you mean a newspaper man?'

'No, ma'am. I'm a writer of novels, several score of them for a fact,' he apologised.

'Blow me down – a literary gentleman! So

we're getting culture as well as cash?'

Clem's cheeks coloured. 'No, no! They're quite humble works, scarcely ever running to more than thirty thousand words. The material is published every week in standardised covers for a mass audience and sells at very low cost.'

'Ah! Let's not make bones about it, darling.' Lucia had seen light. 'You must be talking about them dime novels.'

Clem nodded unhappily.

'Well, I never–!' She looked dubious. 'Can't say as I ever saw the name Conway on any though.'

'I write under an alias,' Clem said stiffly.

'Go on!'

'Yes. It was my publisher's idea that I should be called Nate Ironhorn.'

Lucia laughed. 'Spare us the blushes, darling! That *is* a name I've seen, and I hear it's an amazingly lucrative trade.'

Clem looked morose. 'It is when the creative juices run freely,' he confessed. 'But of late, inspiration has escaped me. What I need is an authentic Western character whom I can develop as the hero of a new series of genuine blood-and-thunder exploits. Which is why I'm going to Hellyer's Creek.'

'Pardon?' Lucia was quite thrown.

'I hear your town marshal is the legendary Virgil Lyons – the "Lion of the Law" as he was one time known.'

Lucia narrowed her eyes thoughtfully. 'Of course, Marshal Lyons,' she murmured. 'A very good friend of my husband and a peace officer of sterling quality, I'm sure…'

'Good God, yes! The very personification of all that is just and good and American. Civil War hero, former member of the Dodge City police, tamer of trail-herd towns and Gold Rush settlements. What a man! With luck, he'll allow me to become his biographer and I shall have a new Buffalo Bill!'

Lucia found in all this a certain hidden, faint amusement, it seemed. She forced herself not to smile. 'Why, I guess we've only known Marshal Lyons in his – er – latter days. Since he's been getting on in years, you know.'

'Lyons a friend of Mr Sanders, you say? Lordsakes, this is a stroke of luck! Do you think I can impose on you to secure me an introduction?'

Lucia conceded to see what could be done, and Clem declared himself much obliged. But that was all else that passed between them before the unmistakable crash of a rifle shot reverberated in the emptiness of the bleak terrain.

More shots rang out. Terrible cries rent the air. And the coach lurched into a sudden burst of speed, pitching Clem to its floorboards.

The man who rode shotgun was as bothered as Whip O'Reilly about the valuable cargo that weighed down the handsome stage he was wont to call disrespectfully their 'dust wagon'.

Fifty thousand dollars was one hell of a lot

of coin.

Outside of other considerations the load lowered the coach body's centre of gravity in the cradle of six-ply leather belts that were its suspension. The vehicle was no longer a live thing, responding to the turns and dips of the trail. It juddered and jarred and swayed alarmingly. Once all that weight was in lateral motion on the sharper curves, it sometimes seemed the stage wouldn't recover at all, but would actually capsize or shatter an expertly crafted wheel into its components of mortised spokes and rim and hand-forged Norway iron.

The shotgun guard was therefore constantly on edge, ready to jump lest he might otherwise be pitched willy-nilly to certain death.

Ten mile out of Tucson, his aggravated mind gathered up a fresh burr. He screwed up his face against the bright light and tried to make out a sight he wasn't sure of. Something was behind them, stirring dust. Not much, but the kind of plume that might be put up by a single horseman.

The dust sign stayed right there, mile after mile, pacing them. Always just out of sight, around a foothill, behind a stand of timber, down in a valley. Never getting any closer.

It made the guard more than a mite twitchy. A lone rider should have easily overtaken them. He was like to hanging back deliberately, the guard reckoned. So he kept his eyes peeled, glued on that 'dust devil' – alert, he thought, to trouble. Some-one was playing an odd game for sure, but with his shotgun to hand he was ready to trump whatever card fell from the unknown hand.

As a consequence, when trouble did strike, he didn't see it until far too late, because it came with startling suddenness from a totally different direction.

The straining horses were hauling the coach up a steep grade that carried the road through a pass between two huge sandstone buttes. Two horsemen nudged their mounts from out behind the cover of each butte and weaved swiftly between the clumps of prickly pear and mesquite dotting the bald side of the mountain.

The four announced their arrival with gunfire.

That the ambushers were masked with bandanas was a seeming irrelevance, lest it was for intimidation and the achievement of a more rapid capitulation. For their intentions were murderous.

A Winchester repeater bucked against the shoulder of one of the gang who rode with reins caught up at his knee.

The whining slug toppled the shotgun guard. Looking to the rear, he never knew what was happening before he bit the trail dust, blood spurting from his holed chest. Then he didn't have the time left to him for even a gabbled prayer. One strangled cry bubbled bloodily from his lips and that was his last.

The ambushers were quickly alongside the coach, within hand-gun range. They slammed off wild shots at the pair riding the box.

The sticky atmosphere was all at once thickened with the belch of flame and lead. A crack of fear opened up in the stony face of the Wells Fargo courier. With a snarl he went for his own shooting iron. It was the last decision and the last move he made before his brain exploded inside his bullet-shattered skull. A violent wave of redness was succeeded by a blackness that was absolute and never-ending.

One of the ambushers was bellowing something incomprehensible to the stage driver, presumably ordering him to stop.

'Git goin', or yuh perish!' Whip O'Reilly roared at his horses. 'Run fer it!'

He fed leather to the team, lashing them desperately into a plunging, breakneck, white-eyed run.

2

The Hired Gun

Joshua Dillard rode the trail to Hellyer's Creek with no great enthusiasm. A one-horse, two-bit, no-account place he'd been told in Tucson before he'd headed out in the tracks of the westbound stage.

But the choice wasn't his to make. When his gun was for hire he roamed pretty much where he pleased. But at this time the gun – a workmanlike, black-gripped .45 calibre 1873 Colt Peacemaker – was already hired. So he went where the job took him. It was too late to get fussy.

And what the hell? Badmen were badmen whenever and wherever they might raise their ugly heads. From Dillard, they got short shrift. He was a hunter, and his hunting was for men. One time – a long ways back, it seemed – he'd been an operative with the famous Allan Pinkerton Detective Agency. In his heart all he'd wanted was a living, spiced with some excitement and adventure. But a sparkling-eyed, peachy-cheeked wench had made counter-claims on that heart and he'd taken her for a wife.

It was then he'd found out that thief-taking and wife-taking didn't mix...

To cut a gut-wrenching, life-shattering story short, he was perforce a free agent, a soldier of fortune hating all lawbreakers with what amounted to obsession. In the cold years alone, he'd grown lean and very hard from an assortment of shrewdly chosen labours. Most of these had ended in blood and turmoil, yet never quite his own death.

So the poignant memories of what he'd lost rode on with him, a haunting presence never to be shrugged off.

Now the trail dust clogged the creases of his brush-clawed clothes like grey gunpowder and was gritty in the light blue of his far-seeing range-rider's eyes. But he paid that and the searing heat no mind. He rode tall in the saddle with straight back and square shoulders, and an air of competence and dignity not lost in the apparent shabbiness of his garb.

He slowed his willing chestnut mare to a clop-clopping walk. A near-imperceptible pressure of the knees, a head-lifting tug of the reins was enough to signal his purpose.

'They ain't to see us, ol' gal,' he murmured. 'The lie of it don't call for no ramping and raging, I savvy.'

Joshua Dillard reflected that this was an affair in which obscurity was a prerequisite to effectiveness. Calling attention to his presence and his allotted function would almost certainly be the end of it – and to the profit that should accrue to his account.

His wary progress came to a rude end when gunfire echoed back from the mountains that rose in a series of saw-toothed ridges ahead. The eventuality of an armed attack on the stage was not one he'd entirely discounted. From the tales he'd heard told, these parts were home to all manner of vermin. Tall stories and lies apart, road agents could be expected to figure among their outcast number.

But to maintain his low profile he'd taken the risk. The galling perception that his tactics might contain cost rather than profit bored uncomfortably into his thoughts.

He had to get going quickly! He pressed heels urgently into the chestnut's flanks and slapped its rump with a big flat hand.

'We gotta ride faster than bats outa hell, Polly!' he grunted abstractedly as though to himself. The mare obediently shot away like a racehorse from the start line.

Ahead, more shots snapped viciously and the dust cloud that marked the passage of the stage was stirred into a brew of turbulence that twisted up into the blue.

Tendrils of unease churned Joshua's innards.

The stage hurtled down trail on slewing wheels from the twin buttes that marked the head of the pass and the place of its deadly ambush. The road dropped with sharp turns and on perilous cambers toward the bottom of a gulch littered with broken rocks and filled with sweltering heat like some ante-pit of hell.

Guttural cries pursued the stage's racketing passage. 'Pull up, jehu! Lift 'em, mister – lift 'em!'

Whip O'Reilly knew he was a dead man. The crudely masked men, he figured, were Butch Simich and his gang. He'd heard the bar-room talk they were operating in the territory, skirting the edges of Marshal Lyons' bailiwick. Simich was bad medicine; too half-baked to make the big league along with the brothers James or Younger, but able to hand out the rough stuff with the worst of them.

The pickings on a stage to Hellyer's Creek weren't like to attract Simich's brand of reckless opportunism in the ordinary run of things. Had he, then, gotten word of the secret Wells Fargo shipment?

O'Reilly's flight was an act of stubborn bravado. 'Plumb loco,' he snarled into his whiskers. 'But I dunno … when a feller's gotta do somep'n', reckon he jest goes ahead an' does it! More'n that, it's Mrs Sanders an' thet thar city boy… Me bein' kinda responsible for 'em.'

In the end, O'Reilly succeeded only in altering the immediate cause of his own death.

The coachmakers had assembled running gear that was the sturdiest and most reliable possible. But their painstaking craft was no proof against the punishment meted out by O'Reilly's wild run from the outlaws.

The stage slithered and swayed drunkenly. Then the offside front wheel crashed into a boulder that had rolled onto the trail from the eroded side of the ravine.

The effect was shattering. The thick iron tyre sprang off. Loosened mortised joints gave way and fell, spokes and hub parted company in a splintering explosion of seasoned oak. Pieces of the yellow-painted lumber, decorated with elegant red pin-stripes, shot spectacularly in all directions.

The stage slumped and dragged. The hand-forged ironwork was rapidly chipped bare of shiny black enamel and struck sparks from the flinty surface of the road.

The horses whinnied shrilly.

Standing on the forward boot, flourishing his whip, O'Reilly never stood a chance. The first jolting impact threw him from his perch.

He hit the hard road headfirst. Arms and legs folded down untidily on top of his body. Broken-necked, he made no move to straighten his unnatural sprawl.

Simich and his three comrades clattered past him and up to the wrecked and halted stage. They whooped obscenely like savage redmen. But mercifully, one of them saw fit to slash loose the four horses, whose piteous shrieks of panic had risen to a new pitch. Freed from their harness and eyes rolling wildly, three of the team cantered off skittishly. The fourth, uttering the most bloodcurdling of the cries, had broken a leg and was shot in the head where it was trying to stand.

Simich leaped down from his silver-horned Mexican saddle. Beneath the masking bandana he was a lean-faced, black-eyed man with a parrot's beak of a nose. He strode up on high-heeled boots to survey the capsized coach, lodged against the rocks amidst a cloud of settling dust.

The leather curtains still swung in the glassless window frames. The steam-shaped poplar side panels were stove in, multiple coats of spar varnish and dark paint cracked and flaked. One lifted wheel kept spinning on its axle, though ever more slowly.

A cruel bark of laughter ripped from the thin lips beneath the outlaw leader's mask, puffing out the saliva-stained cloth. He gestured back down the trail.

'Dead! Every man jack of 'em,' he rasped. 'That stupid ol' man didn't even cost us no slug. Gettin' our hands on this whackin' heap o' *dinero* was easier than gettin' 'em up a saloon trollop's skirts!'

Sycophantic sniggers greeted the crude witticism. It was then he heard a woman's whimper followed by a man's groan.

'Hey, Butch!' ejaculated one of his band. 'Sounds like this caboose's got *passengers!*'

Simich wrenched open the buckled door, six-shooter still swinging in his loose grasp. 'By God, yuh're right!'

Lucia Marques gave a scream of terror and pushed at the jammed door on the far side of the coach.

Clem Conway tried to haul himself groggily off the floor. In a snug shoulder holster he carried an old .36 calibre Navy model Colt. It was a recent, precautionary acquisition with which he'd achieved a level of competence under shooting-gallery conditions in the Bowery. But he didn't fancy his chances enough to attempt a draw against the desperado who glowered at him with smouldering black eyes and already had a gun in his fist.

Another outlaw peered across his chief's shoulder. 'Say, Butch, ain't that the Sanders dame in thar?'

Simich let loose a string of muttered profanities.

Clem reckoned he was more than a mite put out and was wavering over his course of action. Maybe there was still some gallantry in the West after all. Could this roughneck have principles?

'Surely you aren't going to shoot an innocent woman in cold blood?' he appealed.

'Shut yore smarmy trap, mister!'

Of his own fate Clem had no doubt. Like the shotgun guard and the Wells Fargo messenger, he would be ruthlessly dispatched. Half an ounce of lead between the eyes … and despite the cussing owlhoot's seeming quandary he didn't think it would be much longer in coming.

Clem broke out in another sweat. A cold sweat. Any moment now, he assessed, the man called Butch would come to terms with his surprise and uncertainty – and for Clement P. Conway, alias Nate Ironhorn, a slug saying 'The End' would be cast.

One instant everything was deathly still and quiet like in a tableau, then approaching hoofs were beating a tattoo of urgency.

Inside the coach, Clem could see nothing of the newcomer, but he saw Simich wheel round, leveling his weapon. Then it span from his hand with the crash of a gunshot married to the solid thunk of lead on iron.

Clem caught a glimpse of the unseen marksman as he thundered past on a chestnut horse.

Sounds of confusion and wrath and a scrambling for mounts reached his astonished ears.

'Get 'im! Back-shoot the bastard, boys!' came Simich's outraged cry. He clutched his wrenched wrist.

'Sure thing!'

'We'll give 'im blue murder, boss!'

The stage passengers marked for slaughter and the Wells Fargo cargo ready for the pillaging were no longer the bunch's number one priority, it seemed. Summary execution and greed deferred to more demanding business in the wake of this unexpected affront.

A new player had entered the game, with luck or incredible skill riding on his side.

But would it hold? For a fact, the chips were still stacked high against the two trembling travellers.

3

Runaround

Joshua Dillard, too, knew he'd taken on some rugged odds. He'd passed the spread-eagled bodies of the three men who'd ridden the outside of the stagecoach. These owlhoots meant business and no mistake. A corpse or two more was likely to be a matter of shrugging indifference to them.

Their interest would lie in the Wells Fargo sacks and boxes he'd spied being loaded surreptitiously aboard the stage at the depot in Tucson.

The pursuit of his own mission would be best served in the first instance by drawing them off. But his tactics needed fine calculation. The gang could tire of the chase. Or his own death might end it. Then they would return to the stage and his effort would have been for nothing.

All the while he pressed his mare to the limit, the churn of bleak thoughts occupied his mind. Sooner or later he would need to swing back to return to the proper defence of the helpless pair they'd left in the wrecked coach.

To his grim satisfaction the outlaws wasted precious ground, steadying their mounts to loose off rifle shots. The lead sang past him viciously but didn't hit.

The best part of ten minutes was drummed hell-bent up trail, drawing away, before Joshua came upon landscape that remotely set up the chance he was looking for.

Ahead of him the trail entered an ascending defile. To his left the ground pitched away into a steep-sided *arroyo* that continued the path of the defile back on a near-parallel course to the piece of road he'd just travelled.

'You're a sure-footed cayuse, Polly,' he muttered. 'This is where we stump 'em!'

He turned the chestnut off the trail and

jumped a dense fringe of grass and shrubs. Ears forward, the horse trotted and slithered down the precarious slope of the bank. One hoof wrong and it would be all up for them.

'Easy, gal,' Joshua coaxed. 'Make like a mountain goat!'

The manoeuvre paid off. Soon they were doubling back along the bottom of the *arroyo,* effectively screened from the stage road.

Above him, Joshua heard the Simich gang gallop past precipitously, still expending their breath on baying foul oaths and imprecations.

How he hated such buzzard-brained dolts! But the American West had its share of them and more. When the time was ripe, it would afford him a measure of relief from the demons that drove him to wipe out this particular nest of scum. But he also had a living to earn and he recognised that his vendetta against the lawless was a luxury he could indulge in only judiciously.

For now, he was seriously outnumbered and other parties' lives were at risk. He didn't doubt that once they realised they'd lost his trail, these brash owlhooters' heads would cool and they would return to the stage they'd ambushed.

He moved through the *arroyo* cautiously – clear blue eyes searching, rugged face set in hard planes, brain throbbing with a whole round-up of projections. He had some time on his side now, but not much. A fellow couldn't afford to slacken. Anxious to get back to the trail, he dismounted and led the horse up a slanting, rubble-strewn slope where the weather-eaten bank of the *arroyo* had caved in.

On firmer footing, he checked the cinch, climbed into the leather and tore back to the smashed stage.

Clem and Lucia had extricated themselves from the wreckage and were pondering their plight.

The New Yorker greeted Joshua Dillard's reappearance with relief. 'Hell of a business this,' he said. 'I and Miss Marques – or should I say Mrs Sanders? – are deeply grateful for your intervention.'

'Quit the purty speechifying, feller!' Joshua snapped. He tugged his Winchester from the scabbard slung under the stirrup leathers and dropped from the saddle. 'While we're yammering them rannihans'll be heading back to pick up where they left off.'

Lucia gasped. 'You mean, it isn't over?'

'Reckon not, ma'am. An' we ain't all of us gonna ride out on one bronc, so we need a place for holing up.'

Clem straightened his steel-rimmed glasses and cast his gaze around. All he saw was an alien, hostile environment – bare, sun-bleached rock and sparse outcrops of scrubby, brownish vegetation. Nothing suggested a defensive position to his book-taught mind. He elected to appear philosophical.

'Then our goose is cooked anyway, it seems.'

Joshua could understand his feelings, but he hadn't retrieved the situation so far just to let it slip out of his hands without a fight.

'Mebbe. But we can't move far without them catching us. I suggest we stick around the stage.' He slewed his head round and nodded. 'Behind them rocks it's lodged against is as good a place as any.'

Clem smiled thinly. 'And it'll enable you to keep a sharp eye on what happens to all the money it carries!'

'What's that supposed to mean, feller?' Joshua challenged.

'Well, I don't imagine your coming on the scene was entirely fortuitous, sir, if you follow my drift. Despite the roughness of your dress, I'll wager you'd be an agent for Wells Fargo.'

Joshua shrugged. 'Think what you like, mister. There ain't no one to take on your bet anyhows.'

Abruptly, he slapped Polly's rump and took Lucia's arm and hustled her in the direction he'd indicated.

The horse took itself a short way off across a slope sparsely given to grama grass and into the limited shade cast by a clump of straggly, high-grown juniper.

Lucia stared into the stranger's hard brown face uncertainly. She was a woman who'd done a lot of reading of men's expressions in her time. What she saw, dust-stained and tense, persuaded her that if anyone could be relied on in a tight spot like this, it would be a man like this one. The stiffness went out of her and, gathering up her long skirts, she allowed herself to be led.

She said throatily, 'I entrust myself entirely in your hands, Mr – er–'

'Dillard, ma'am.'

Joshua hunkered down amongst the rocks, unceremoniously pushing Lucia into a handy hollow behind him.

Clem joined them, dragging the Navy Colt from his shoulder holster. He hadn't intended to alienate the man who'd almost certainly saved their lives – so far.

'I might be able to put in my two bits,' he

said by way of apology, and gestured with the handgun.

'You can use that thing?' Joshua asked incredulously.

'I – I think so. If I was minded to.'

Joshua snorted. 'You'll use it. Them *pistoleros* ain't gonna be coming back for no genteel picnic.'

He got himself lying flat, loaded rifle at the ready, and peered through the heat mirage that swam over the hot rocks, his eyes slitted against the harsh glare of the sun.

It didn't take Butch Simich and his partners long to realise Dillard had given them the slip – and where their most profitable interests lay. They pounded back into the gulch noisily.

'The goddamn stage is wrecked,' Simich grated. 'We got work on our hands packhorsin' out thet *dinero*.' His face, now unmasked, was red and sweaty; his temper black.

'Thar's worse work, boss … like punchin' cows an' bustin' sods an' splittin' rocks.

Let's get stuck in!'

But the speaker was doing no more work, ever. The minute he swung out of the saddle and took his first stride toward the wreckage, Joshua Dillard put him down.

The heavy .44 slug from the Winchester knocked him writhing to the ground. His three *compadres* scattered instantly at the booming report, spurring their horses for cover amid jumbled rocks on the far slope of the gulch.

'Bloody hell!' a voice raged.

Two more shots followed hard on the heels of the first. The horse beneath Butch Simich reared with a squealing whinny. He grabbed wildly at the showy silver saddle horn, but then kicked his feet free of the stirrups as the animal crashed over sideways, throwing him heavily. He rolled to his feet and, head down, hunted cover fast.

Simich was crazy-mad. 'We bin dry-gulched! Thet sneaky sonofabitch musta doubled back!'

'Whadya gonna do?' a fleeing sidekick

jerked, his face flint-white.

A fourth and fifth shot raked the dust close by Simich's boots. He ducked behind a big boulder. 'Do?' he roared. 'We're gonna pour lead on the stinkin' bastard, thet's what! Two can play at his game. When he shows his face, he loses it, jest like Howie there.'

His two surviving companions hurriedly dropped from the mounts that made them high, clear targets and went to earth among the rocks.

'Gimme cover!' Simich barked at the man crouched nearest him. 'I gotta get my saddle gun.'

He crawled back ignominiously through the dirt, careful to keep the bulk of his dead horse between himself and their hidden assailant. Shots screamed over his head. But he made it there and back again. He bared his teeth in a wolfish snarl as a last slug hit the boulder that was his shelter, showering him with dust and sharp splinters of rock.

'We'll make buzzard bait outa the interferin' sticky bill!' he blazed.

'What about Sanders' missus, boss?' he was reminded. 'Guess she an' the city gent must be in there with 'im.'

A drifting pall of gunsmoke marked Joshua Dillard's position behind the abandoned stage. Simich gave his inquirer a brief, cold look. He levered a shell into his carbine's breech, threw it to his shoulder and squeezed the trigger. The gun blasted and bucked.

As if on cue, Lucia Marques' scream pierced the hot dry air, amplified in the natural amphitheatre of the gulch.

Simich licked his lips. 'Guess yuh're right,' he said, a nervousness breaking his voice. 'Damn' curious turn-up... We'll hold fire till they have to light out, then we'll move in.'

'It's a standoff,' Joshua surmised. 'Seems like they got some compunction 'bout driving us out with undirected bullets. Wal, we can play the waiting game likewise.'

Clem nodded eagerly. 'When the coach

47

fails to arrive in Hellyer's Creek, a search party will be sent out. Why, I'm sure the bank will insist. And Mrs Sanders' husband will be jumping up and down–'

Lucia cut in, shaking her head sadly. 'Uh-uh. Daniel isn't expecting me till tomorrow. You see, I was coming back from my trip a day early…'

'Oh, said Clem, puzzled. 'Tucson not to your liking?'

'It wasn't that, dearie. I was figuring on catching Dice by surprise.'

'Ah, how nice!'

'Not if I'd caught him fooling around with percentage girls, it wouldn't have been.'

'Percentage–? Oh yes, the saloon employees.' Clem crimsoned at his lack of perspicacity and Lucia's worldliness.

Joshua smiled to himself wryly. The Easterner was likeable enough but wet behind the ears, he thought. It didn't make his job easy.

But Clem was not crushed for long. 'I have it!' he exclaimed not many moments later.

Lucia, considerably brightened since the

cessation of gunfire, turned her bold eyes back to him.

'We must share it, darling,' she gurgled. 'Unless it's an infectious disease.'

'One of us must make a dash for Mr Dillard's horse and ride for help,' he said simply.

Joshua's jaw dropped a fraction. 'You're talking foolish, boy,' he drawled grimly. 'I can't leave you to protect Mrs Sanders an' the Wells Fargo money. 'Sides, they'd cut me down before I was in the saddle!'

Clem grinned ruefully. 'No – you don't understand. *I* would ride out and you would give me covering fire,' he said earnestly. 'I've ridden a horse before, you know.'

'Forget it!' Joshua exploded. 'This ain't some fancy New York estate around here, y' know. A tenderfoot wouldn't get five mile, even without one o' them gunhawks on his tail.'

Clem was put out. 'Maybe you have a better idea,' he suggested with a scowl.

'No, I ain't. But if you're gonna die, I ain't

allowing no flaming suicide!'

For several seconds they stared at each other in silence, then Clem shrugged and settled back into a new position to ease his cramped limbs.

'This could drag on for hours,' he said. 'Until those desperadoes know assistance is on its way to us, they'll be prepared to sit and wait for your Wells Fargo money.'

Lucia swallowed. 'We'll need water, food, Mr Dillard.'

'So will they,' he replied uncompromisingly.

'No doubt they have canteens with them,' Clem pointed out, 'and they could spare one of their number to go fetch anything else they need.'

'We'll see,' Joshua growled. 'You aren't throwing no scare into me.'

Lucia sighed. 'Oh, I *do* like a determined man!'

Joshua told her coolly, 'The next way station can't be no more 'n ten – fifteen mile down the trail. They'll be starting to wonder for sure. Mebbe they'll send a rider.'

His conclusion amused Lucia. 'From Pennydale Ford?' she scoffed with a bitter laugh. 'Why, the station master there's an old soak. Like as not he doesn't know what *day* it is unless his daughter's told him!'

Joshua's brows lowered in a deep frown at the news. 'Then that ain't so good. I guess we'll have to learn patience, ma'am.'

But the stalemate was to last less than one more hour.

4

A Cyclone with Red Hair

'Well, Mr Conway, you're certainly getting some first-hand excitement,' Lucia ventured with a nervous smile.

'More than I'd bargained for and at closer quarters.' Clem shuddered. 'The next death could be yours or mine!'

'Hush your yap, willya!' Joshua flagged a hand for silence but didn't turn from his vigilant watch of the rocks that sheltered the outlaw gang.

'Mr Dillard!' Clem began huffily. 'I don't like your–'

Then he broke off, for he heard it, too.

A puff of hot breeze rustled the dry grasses that poked up from the cracks. And blown along on the breath of it, another sound came to the ears of the trapped trio.

'Hoofbeats!' Clem exclaimed.

'Help is at hand!' Lucia cried dramatically.

Joshua Dillard's lips twisted cynically. 'Jest one rider, ma'am,' he reported. 'A start, I'll allow, but them jaspers across the way are gonna hear same as us.'

'You believe they'll interfere!'

'With bullets, Mr Conway! Why ever not? They've already killed three men to pull off this caper.' Joshua's tone was laconic.

Clem waved his Colt. 'The range is a bit far for a revolver to do much good, but I must help you put up covering fire. These swine can't be allowed to attack innocent folks.'

'Damned right, Mr Conway.'

Lucia shivered. 'It makes me go cold to think that man out there might be riding unwittingly toward his death!'

Whatever each of them expected – complication, salvation or both – the rider's appearance at the head of the gulch brought a total surprise.

'Good God! It's a woman!' said Clem.

'Watch out,' yelled Joshua.

Simultaneously, two rifles crashed.

A low-crowned stetson flew from the head of the startled horsewoman, holed through the brim. The mop of carrot-red hair tucked under it burst free – along with a virulent oath that would have blued the air in a Tombstone bar-room.

The Simich henchman who'd raised himself to fire was toppled back like a tenpin among his cohorts, blood seeping into his bullet-torn shirtsleeve.

The girl's horse, a spirited black pony, reared, but the rider didn't attempt to control it. She plunged expertly from the saddle and rolled across the dusty trail. She went fast, making no effort to regain her feet till she could dart in among the rocks.

As a crowning act of bravado, she then snatched a six-shooter from the low-slung belt that circled her slim, jeans-clad hips and loosed off several shots, having accurately picked the direction of her attacker.

The Simich bunch was seemingly stunned into passivity. No further fire came from their position.

Clem Conway was lost in admiration. 'Good Lord! That was a spunky recovery!'

'Coupled with a streak o' luck an' a hell of a nerve,' commented Joshua.

'Who can the girl be? She should be in a Wild West show!'

'I know her,' cut in Lucia. 'That kid's Dorothy-May from the way station. Old Ezra Pennydale's gel.'

'Kid' seemed hardly the right word, Clem thought, from the confident way she carried herself across to the group pinned down behind the stage. But as she drew near he saw she was probably still in her teens, a slightly bony, leggy figure with freckles spattered brightly like orange paint flecks across her face.

She wore men's clothes careless, it seemed, of convention, fashion or condition. The jeans were made from home-spun cloth and showed little evidence of patching or mending but much of hard wear, including a few rips and tears. Buttons were missing from the faded plaid shirt. Her riding boots were heavily scuffed and out at the right toe.

She jerked a thumb at the smashed-up stagecoach. 'Did that gunslingin' trash do this, too?' she asked, green eyes aglitter.

''Sright. Get your head down, miss,' advised Joshua. 'It must stand out like a beacon an' next time you're liable to get it blasted clean offa your shoulders.'

Dorothy-May glowered but complied. 'I told my old man the westbound was god-awful late, but he was kinda – uh – incapacitated, so I came out a-lookin' my own self.' Her sandy brows knit thoughtfully. 'What were they after, mister?'

'The usual,' Joshua clipped.

'Fifty thousand dollars in Wells Fargo money bound for the bank at Hellyer's Creek,' said Clem, who could see no reason for rudeness or secrecy.

'Hell's bells! An' y'mean to say they sent along a li'le bankin' feller like you to look after it?'

'Oh, no, there was another man from Wells Fargo. I'm not a *banker*.'

'What gives with the funny store clothes then?' she demanded, wrinkling her freckled nose at Clem's crumpled pinstripe suit.

'Mr Conway is an author, child!' said Lucia. 'He is the famous Nate Ironhorn.'

'What! You're joshin' me.'

Clem wriggled with embarrassment. 'Just the odd book to make a living, you know.'

'But them yarns are *won'erful*. I've read *Deadshot Dan, King of the Border Men* a hun'red times!' She shook her red head in amazement at her favourite writer's appearance. 'Wal, you're quite diff'rent from anythin' I imagined…'

In truth, she was instantly seeing Clem in a changed, much more favourable light. Nate Ironhorn's orange-covered dime novels were in her estimation masterpieces worthier than the works of William Shakespeare.

But more urgent matters had to be addressed. 'So where's this Wells Fargo feller?

And Whip O'Reilly and the shotgun guard?' she enquired.

'Dead! All three of 'em – in the dust back up the trail,' spat Joshua, mincing no words.

Dorothy-May flinched, but only slightly.

'Mr Dillard here is holding the ruffians off till the forces of law and order arrive,' said Clem. 'We'd only the one Winchester and one saddle horse, you see. And he wouldn't let me make a break and ride for Hellyer's Creek.'

He added the last apologetically, but Dorothy-May instantly leapt on his words. 'I should reckon not, fer God's sake! You're jest a greenhorn an' all, despite all them grand adventures you've writ! Now me, I know the back trails an' all the tricks. I kin git the scum goin' in circles like hound dawgs chasin' their tails.'

Joshua spared her a sidelong glance, his cool eyes taking in the lithe, athletic fitness of her and the determined lift of her chin. She wasn't much more than a slip of a girl, but why not? She'd already shown herself daring and capable. She knew the country and she sounded as though she might know what was what.

She was their best chance.

Her black pony had frisked off, trailing its reins, to join Joshua's chestnut by the junipers.

'If you're to fetch reinforcements, you'll need your cayuse. How'd you get it back?' Joshua said by way of a noncommittal acceptance of her implied offer.

'She'll come,' the girl said confidently. 'Jest make sure them mangy curs don't up an' shoot her!'

She suddenly put her fingers to her lips and a piercing, whistling call, like the cry of a bird, split the air.

The pony tossed its head and came instantly at a canter. Maybe the outlaws were as astonished as Clem and Lucia, for they let the beast join the opposing party without hindrance.

Colt in hand, Dorothy-May swung aboard the black behind the cover of the stage and the rocks. 'Don't fret yourself none, Mr Conway-Ironhorn, thet posse ull be here in two jumps – wal, afore sundown anyways!'

As she broke into the open, Butch Simich rushed out to intercept her, a six-shooter drawn.

Joshua Dillard swore mightily, fearful to shoot lest he hit the girl or her mount.

Simich fired straight at Dorothy-May's red head. Or where it had been. For she was all at once stretched low along the horse's neck, heading straight for him, her own revolver extended.

Her green eyes were ablaze with impish malice.

She triggered off a wild shot as the horse almost rode Simich down. The gun went off that close to his head the crimson flash of it near blinded him and the report was deafening. Scorched by the burning powder, he stumbled back in utter confoundment, crashing into his two flabbergasted followers.

In just a few seconds, Dorothy-May had hit them like a cyclone and was gone.

The house was the finest in Hellyer's Creek, a two-storey frame with tall, shuttered windows and wide verandahs both front and back. It was painted a spotless, glaring white. For a decade or more it had been the home of the pioneer Hellyer family, founders of the settlement and respected general merchants.

Of late it had been occupied by the man who had procured most of the contrastingly tatty Main Street properties along with it.

Daniel 'Dice' Sanders favoured the house as his residence because it represented an unmistakable symbol of his status as the uncrowned king of Hellyer's Creek. Its acquisition from the former owners had proven to the locals beyond doubt that he'd arrived. But just as importantly it was conveniently situated across the alley from the back door of the Silver Buckle Saloon, the palace of vulgar pleasures that was the cornerstone of Sanders' recent fortunes.

Even now, he was taking full advantage of that convenience to exercise his own pleasure while keeping a fat, beringed finger close to the pulse of his small-town empire.

What had started as a handy bolthole for Sanders had turned into a prison *de luxe*. Boredom with Hellyer's Creek and all it stood for had to be alleviated somehow. Hence added reason for the constant procession of percentage girls that passed through his saloon. The girls were often imported from San Francisco, his former stamping ground as a professional gambler where he still had connections as well as enemies.

Sanders was an insatiable sampler of his own wares.

'What a lovely home you have, Dice,' said his bleach-blonde companion as she rolled her well-rounded figure free across the showy expanse of a feather-mattressed bed. 'So much nicer than that hot little room back of your office... When does Lucia return?'

Pouched little hog's eyes peered out shiftily from beneath the saloon-keeper's hairless brows. What was it this girl brought to her work? Artlessness, honesty or hard-headed practicality?

'Not till tomorrow, my dove,' wheezed Sanders, who despite the room's comparative coolness was sweating freely from his exertions. 'But let's not think of my wife, Cora; she doesn't understand me,' he added. The stale excuse dropped moistly from his thick red lips, as burnt-out as the soggy Havana cigar butt he'd discarded into a cut-glass ashtray at the bedside.

She rolled back to him, plastered kisses and more rouge on his shiny bald pate, and her deft hands roamed. 'Sugar pie,' she murmured; stupid lard-barrel, she thought. But she knew it would be a fool thing to buck power and money.

He chuckled rumblingly deep down in his bloated white belly.

Then an inert flaccidity reclaimed him with the sudden transfer of his interest to matters outside. A pounding of urgent hoofs disturbed the hot afternoon somnolence of Hellyer's Creek.

Unwrapping himself from Cora's enticing

limbs, he heaved his fleshy bulk off the groaning bed with surprising alacrity. He shrugged into a blue silk robe.

'What is it, Dice?' Cora asked, assuming a hurt pout.

Sanders lumbered over to the open floor-length windows and pushed through the thick red drapes onto a small balcony that jutted out from the upper storey.

'It's someone riding in lickety-spit, an' I think I know why,' he said, a new excitement thickening his voice.

From the balcony he could see a significant slice of Main Street through the gaps between the buildings that flanked it and across the vacant lot beside his saloon. He observed the rider and her lathered black pony.

'Yeah, it's that pants-wearing filly from the stage station at Pennydale Ford an' she's gone pell-mell into the marshal's office,' he reported smugly.

He rubbed his fat, immaculately manicured hands together, and stepped back into the room. Gold glittered from the tooth fillings in his smiling mouth.

Cora sensed she had new and threatening competition for his interest. Her experience of life had educated her in sure ways to recapture wandering male attention. Sitting up, she lifted both hands to straighten her bed-tousled hair, making her back an arch that thrust forward her big breasts in blatant invitation.

Sanders, seeming to see and not to see her at the same time, laughed exultantly. 'This calls for celebration!'

Then he lunged at her, tumbling her deep into the softness of the mattress, his sausage-like fingers groping and probing.

Beneath the crushing grossness of him, she wriggled ineffectually.

'Ow,' she said.

'This is where we can start twisting *their* arms,' said Joshua Dillard. Dorothy-May had just gone from sight round the bend in the trail, and he was squinting along the barrel of his Winchester, waiting for fresh movement from the outlaws' position.

He was tensed for action like a coiled spring, his finger on the rifle trigger.

'I don't quite follow, Mr Dillard,' said Lucia Marques, a blankness registering behind the now-smudged paint of her face.

'This scum was waiting for us to quit or give 'em a chance to eliminate us, so's they could grab the loot outa the wrecked stage. Right?'

'Exactly. And they still are,' said Clem Conway, mopping his sweating brow. 'Thank God they didn't kill that fine girl!'

'But now they ain't able to bide their time,' explained Joshua. 'They gotta make the choice – fork their hosses *pronto* an' catch that gal, or storm us an' shift the haul afore she has a posse out here! Get that Navy Colt good an' ready, Mr Conway!'

The thrust of what Joshua said must have dawned on Simich and company about the same time as it was sinking in with Lucia and Clem.

Yelled orders broke out, then the band made a dash for their three surviving horses. It seemed they'd chosen to pursue Dorothy-May.

Joshua sprang to his feet and threw his rifle to his shoulder. A shell was levered into the breech and he snapped off a rapid shot without hesitation.

The slug failed to hit a target but whined sharply between Simich and one of the other two, causing their nervous horses to shy.

While they struggled to regain control, Joshua darted to a new position, from where he could command the trail out of the gulch, and effectively block pursuit of Dorothy-May.

Clem scurried after him, clutching his derby to his head with one hand and brandishing the old Colt with the other.

'All right, fellers!' Simich raged, seeing how the business was panning out. 'They're askin' fer it – let's get 'em!'

5

Living Legend

'Back!' Joshua shouted at Clem. 'Stick with Mrs Sanders!' Inwardly he cursed the greenhorn's foolhardy courage in rushing out from their cover.

'We have to prevent them from stopping Miss Pennydale!' bleated Clem. 'You said as much yourself!'

''T'ain't no call to end up buzzard bait!'

The exchange was drowned in a staccato burst of revolver fire from the owlhooters.

Clem knew he had to fall back before he was encircled. He dived and rolled into a dip. Bullets pelted his face with dirt and something glanced his temple with an almighty wallop even as he wildly triggered the Navy Colt in reply.

The New Yorker's sudden flop deceived their foes into thinking he was done for. The outlaws dived for shelter themselves, re-lining their weapons on Joshua Dillard. Scarcely knowing what he was doing, Clem lurched to his feet and stumbled back to their old position in a crouch. Black spots swirled in a red haze before his eyes. He heard Joshua's Winchester crashing, and more outlaw slugs skimmed close to his head, going high.

'Mr Conway! Mr Conway!' Lucia Marques cried. 'Oh, you poor man – your head is bleeding!'

Suddenly, she stood up, shaking her fists, her voice rising in a scream.

'You stinking polecats! This man has no quarrel with you! He's a harmless Easterner with no interest in your bloodstained money!'

Her furious outburst reminded Simich and his partners of her presence. It seemed to rock them on their heels.

'Shuddup sister, or we'll blast yuh down!'

Simich growled back from behind a rock, but there was uneasiness in his tone.

Joshua cut in, shouting harshly. 'You fellers are the ones that are gonna eat lead. The girl's got clean away. If you've got any damn' brains, you know you'll be facing a posse if you stick around!'

A mumble of argument ensued amongst the murderers.

Clem strained to pick out the words, but failed. Puzzlingly, they seemed to have no stomach for mounting an attack and pushing the confrontation to a rapid and fatal conclusion.

All at once, they made a second concerted rush for their horses and mounted up.

'There they go!' cried Lucia. 'Quick! Shoot the bastards!'

The Simich gang was already pounding off at a fast gallop.

Joshua shook his head. Bitterness rode the hard, curving gash of his mouth.

'Plumb outa the question, ma'am. This Winchester's fired a whole sixteen shots an'

I ain't carrying no more .44 cartridges. All I had left against them coyotes at this range was bluff!'

He tapped the .45 Colt Peacemaker in his gunbelt. Clem noticed the black grip was worn and scarred with a deep crack. 'My side-arm ain't chambered for the same calibre as the rifle,' Joshua explained.

Clem mopped at the blood streaming down his white face. He felt weak with a relief that bordered on hysteria.

'But we're saved … and your money's saved, too, Mr Dillard. Unless those ungodly vermin should come back.'

'I don't see it, Mr Conway. But that's a messy crease you have. D'you think you can sit a horse? I reckon we should push on to the station at Pennydale Ford an' get it properly cleaned an' dressed.'

'I'll be all right,' Clem muttered.

Lucia abruptly lifted her skirt and tore a strip from her frilled white petticoat. 'Here, let me fix a bandage,' she offered.

Joshua cast his pale eagle gaze over the

landscape, having second thoughts. 'While you're doin' that, mebbe I'll stash the money that ain't locked in the strongbox someplace less obvious.'

Soon he was humping the canvas Wells Fargo sacks from the wreck to a scrub-grown crevasse near where his horse still grazed. The chestnut had now been joined by one of the team cut from the traces that had held them to the stagecoach pole.

After he'd pulled enough scrub over the bulging sacks to meet his satisfaction, Joshua turned his untiring attention to the saddleless horse.

It was no mean feat to climb aboard a strange horse without stirrups, not knowing whether it was broken to anything other than harness. But Joshua did it. And his success told him what he wanted to know.

'This cayuse'll take a rider,' he told the others, who observed his antics. 'My chestnut is an obedient beast. You two can ride her, an' she'll follow where I go.'

Soon they were riding the trail at an easy

jog, headed for Pennydale Ford.

'No sign of the posse, Mr Dillard,' Clem worried. 'I hope no mishap befell that red-haired girl. Do you think the road agents could have had accomplices to waylay her?'

Joshua grinned to himself. 'It's like to be second nature to a feller in your line, Mr Conway,' he said, 'but I reckon you'd be over-exercising that imagination o' your'n.'

From the misty look in Clem's eyes, he also figured Dorothy-May's image had marked itself indelibly on the writer's retinas. That or the crack he'd taken to his skull had affected his wits.

Lucia said, 'The gel knows how to take care of herself, I assure you, darling. Her father's a drunk and she practically runs the way station single-handed. Strong men in Hellyer's Creek go in fear of her sharp tongue, I understand.'

'I don't doubt her capabilities, ma'am,' Clem said huffily. 'But our attackers were the most despicable hellions. Utterly ruthless. And damnit, Miss Pennydale is a *woman!*'

Lucia shrugged. 'Woman enough to have made an impression, it seems,' she said archly.

Colour mounted to Clem's petticoat-bandaged forehead and he fell silent.

Soon after, his fears were put to rest. Dorothy-May was at the forefront of a bunch of oncoming riders. In fact, she heeled her horse slightly ahead of the ostensible leader, a white-moustached man, tall in the saddle, whose vest sported a glint of starred metal.

'By crackity! Whadya do to your head, Ironhorn?' Dorothy-May demanded as she rode up. Her green eyes were wide with alarm.

'I was shot at by the road agents,' Clem said.

'It's just a scraped scalp, miss,' Joshua said. 'But he's lucky. That slug came passing close to spilling his brains.

'Hell was surely a-poppin' when I lit out,' said Dorothy-May. 'I tell yuh, I didn't think they'd quit till we got back or y'all was a-headin' for pearly gates!'

Joshua said ironically, 'I guess me an' my Winchester an' Mr Conway with his Navy Colt must of scared 'em off. They skeedaddled anyways. Mebbe the marshal here can round 'em up *muy pronto*.'

He turned to the lawman. 'I'm Joshua Dillard, formerly with the Pinkertons, sir. I take it you'd be Marshal Virgil Lyons. Like most folk, I know your fine reputation.'

Frankly, despite his outward respect, Joshua was a mite perturbed at his first sight of the old-time town-tamer and troublebuster. He tried to pin down his qualms.

Sure, Lyons was an impressive gent for his years, still straight-backed, and his mane of white hair thick and bushy beneath his hat. But the hazel eyes, shot with yellow, were rheumy and ever-swivelling in their sockets. And the hands that clasped the reins of his bay gelding weren't just gnarled with age – they trembled.

Clem had no such reservations. He saw a living legend: the 'Lion of the Law'. He dismounted from the chestnut, Lucia slipping down ahead of him, and raised his derby in salute.

'I'm honoured to meet you, Marshal Lyons. I'm Clem Conway, a writer from New York, and I hope you'll obli–'

Joshua interrupted. 'Mebbe the privilege o' interviewing Mr Lyons will have to wait for a fitter time an' place,' he said curtly. 'The marshal an' his men have more urgent business with a mob o' stickup artists.'

Lyons' horse shuffled and the man wiggled his bushy white brows and harrumphed.

'Now hold your hosses, mister,' he prevaricated. 'That ain't necessarily so. This strictly speakin' is outa my bailiwick. Them high-tailin' gents is prob'ly to hell an' gone an' the trail colder than a whore's heart at this here juncture...'

Joshua was stunned. 'The owlhoots will have left sign for sure. One of them was bleeding from his arm like a pig,' he argued. He looked around at the wildness of the locality. 'My guess is they'll be holed up in this country someplace. You plan to let 'em

77

get away with armed robbery?'

Lyons bristled. 'Sounds to me like they didn't get to do no robbery.' He eyed Dorothy-May slanchways as though seeking her confirmation on this point.

She hunched a shoulder and rolled her green eyes at the others as if to say she'd done her part as best she could.

'You have some other duty mebbe,' Joshua said, his voice thick with sarcasm.

'Don't go tellin' me m' duty, pup!' the marshal exploded. 'I'm gonna escort these stage passengers to safety.' The idea pleased him. 'Yeah, that's what I'm gonna do – an' my depities are gonna see about collectin' that Wells Fargo shipment.' He sneered. 'Jest in case yuh should hev plans o' your own, Dillard!'

Joshua ignored the insinuation. 'Fine! Mr Conway is a wounded man. If you're taking charge o' arrangements for him, I guess that frees me to track down them owlhoots my own self. They killed three good men, remember? An' I hate killers!'

'Fool's game!' Lyons retorted.

Clem was embarrassed by the exchange.

'Hey! Aren't you being a little high-handed, Mr Dillard?' he asked sheepishly. 'I realise the attack on the stage might be cause for a red face, but you've acquitted yourself well. Mr Lyons is a veteran lawman and I think you should respect his opinions.'

'I ain't giving a damn to his opinions!' Joshua snorted. He dropped to the ground from the stage horse and strode over to his chestnut, which he remounted. 'Seems to me like I'm wasting a passel of time on a tuckered-out ol' coot. *Adios!*'

He wheeled the horse and headed back, dust boiling thickly in his path.

Lyons fumed. 'That gink's gotta hell of a gall, by God! We'll let it go fer now, but if he shows his face in Hellyer's Creek, I'll shovel him more grief'n he kin handle!'

He detailed a section of the posse with two deputies in command to locate the stage and secure its cargo. Before they were dispatched Clem obligingly described how part of the Wells Fargo shipment had been shifted into concealment.

The Pennydale Ford settlement was no more than the last way station before Hellyer's Creek. Typically of its kind, it stood in isolation ten miles from the township and a wearying fifteen or so from its nearest counterpart in the opposite direction.

Relief team stage horses swished lazy tails at flies in a big corral. A yellowish creek flowed past the place sluggishly, and several cottonwoods drew sustenance from the moist earth bordering its curving banks. The station buildings were raw. A stable and outhouses were clapboard; the main building, long and low, was built of adobe.

It was a functional place, passably tidy and clean, but in need of a lick of paint it would probably never get. For already the railroad surveyors had poked their way through the country and in time it was sure to become just another abandoned ruin – a forgotten, crumbling milestone in the history of the frontier.

In the big dining-room Clem regaled the station master's daughter with the official, world view of the local law officer while she – as ever a girl of many parts – competently cleaned and bathed the bullet crease on his bloodied brow.

Through the window, Clem could see the great man himself trying to make himself understood by Dorothy-May's grey and grizzled father, old Ezra Pennydale, whose answers seemed to consist largely of head shakings and broken-toothed grins.

Clem was astounded that Dorothy-May should not be acquainted with the legend of the Lion of the Law.

'But Virgil Lyons once worked as a wrangler for the stage line. Surely your father must have told you how he routed the Navaho horse thieves,' he insisted. 'And you must have heard how his famous gunfight with the dubious Potter brothers ended the family's bloody feud with the Hansons.'

'Nary a word,' said Dorothy-May, shaking her red mophead and dabbing an evil-looking brown tincture on Clem's wound.

'Ouch!' he complained.

'It musta all happened when I was a very li'le gal,' she opined. 'Ain't never know'd our marshal as a "Lion o' the Law" – more like an ol' hoss what shoulda bin put out t' pasture years back. Why, he's the kinda jasper who looks happiest a-sittin' in a rockin' chair on a verandah, I reckon. Ain't no better use than my own ol' man when it comes t' *real* work.'

Clem was horrified at the girl's lack of respect.

'Ah, but you're letting appearances deceive you, Miss Pennydale. Don't you see? Marshal Lyons' reputation would be no secret to the unruly elements, and it's exactly what lets him put his feet up.' He nodded confidently to himself. 'The riffraff are in check; the man is quietly ruling with a rod of iron.'

'Horse dung!' Dorothy-May clipped back. 'If'n anyone rules Hellyer's Creek, it's that damned twister Sanders married t' her yuh was ridin' the stage with from Tucson.'

Clem's eyebrows shot up. 'Hush, girl! There are laws of slander!'

'I'll give yuh a fr' instance,' Dorothy-May ploughed on regardless of his admonition. 'Thar's them Mex squatters what set up in that derelict soddy 'tween here an' town. I ain't got nothin' agin' greasers, but they's always a-troublemakin', an' they ain't scairt o' no Lyons neither. Yuh know why?'

Clem lifted his head. 'The Mexicans have had a hard time of it. War and Border troubles; filibuster raids and poverty. Marshal Lyons is also renowned for his sense of justice and his compassion,' he explained patiently, primly. 'He's *tolerating* the people in this sod house, that's all.'

Dorothy-May laughed aloud, her eyes green sparkles of mirth. 'He's toleratin' 'em, shore nuff! An' I knows fer why. 'Cos thet soddy an' its acres belong t' Dice Sanders, is why. He got it in payment o' gamblin' debts from the last owner. An' he don't c'llect no

83

rent from them Mexes. He swaps 'em cheap rotgut, as much they kin swill, fer the money an' stock an' stuff they beg an' steal from honest folks.'

Clem was bewildered by her knowledgeable plunge into this deep and murky pool of gossip.

'Frankly, I don't follow how this scuttlebuck has any bearing on the discussion.'

Dorothy-May looked at him with withering pity. 'The *dinero,*' she said, extending her hand and rubbing the work-roughened pad of her thumb across her fingertips.

'What *dinero?*'

She frowned darkly. 'The kickbacks thet snaky Sanders slips ol' Lyons fer turnin' a blind eye t' the crooked ways he runs his saloon – the rigged gamin' tables an' all, the painted harpies what lift honest cowpokes' bankrolls.'

'My dear, this is preposterous! I fear you've been reading too many of the overcoloured tales written by my rivals in New York!'

Dorothy-May's temper, finely held in check, at last bubbled over.

'Awright then, mister,' she said, seizing up her tin bowl and slopping pink-stained water onto Clem's pinstriped pants leg. 'Scoff if you like. But it's the honest truth, I tellya! Jest you wait an' see!'

6

Trail into Danger

Joshua Dillard had no trouble following the sign of Butch Simich and his pards. They'd run like a pack of wounded wolves. No trouble had been taken to cover their traces. At least one of them was losing blood. Fresh hoofprints, not yet wind-wiped from the dust, and the like of broken thorn bush added tell-tale testimony.

Caution was called for.

'When a man turns wolf an' finds hisself run smack into a corner, he'll kill an' kill again,' Joshua reminded himself. These men had already proven they were of the killer breed. Their type was a trigger to what had become a gut response in him. He scowled at hurtful memories and bitterness darkened his eyes.

Absently but gently, he coaxed the chestnut mare on.

The owlhoots' track took Joshua on an ascending trail that was hardly more than an ill-defined bridle path. They'd made no attempt to hightail it hell-for-leather down the main stage road out of the territory. Soon he'd reached wild mountain escarpments, trekking into ever rougher country. The vegetation changed with the altitude. The less bleak slopes were timbered with pine. Ahead, ragged peaks rose, canyon-gashed, remote and gloomy as the sun sank westwards, lengthening the welcome shadows.

'Going to earth, I reckon, Polly, an' someplace purty near.'

Joshua rode through a brushy gap between two pine-topped ridges, mindful that he was pushing the mare to the limits of endurance. He was about to make a stop for rest when he thought he heard another horse whinny.

Instantly, Joshua pulled up the chestnut's drooping neck and thrust a hand forward over the patient beast's distending nostrils to deter an answering nicker.

'Hush, Polly,' he warned softly.

His pale gaze raked the shadowy heights around him; found nothing.

Maybe it was time to rest his horse anyway. He swung down and left Polly standing obediently with the reins on the ground between two boulders that thrust up jaggedly out of the brush.

Joshua went forward on foot, stealthy as an Indian. Beyond the gap and over a hummock, the terrain sloped gently downwards and into a hollow, not unlike a huge bowl, and this was half-filled with forest growth.

It was also the site of what might once have been a line-camp. There were several shacks and one more substantial structure – a cabin, which looked in a state of partial decay with moss creeping up from the ground on the north side onto the lower logs of its walls.

Occupation was evidenced by a motley assortment of horseflesh occupying one of several pole corrals.

Joshua ghosted into scratchy cover and his hand drifted close to his hip and the reassuring bulk of the well-oiled, loaded six-gun that rested there in greased leather. He was braced for trouble. Silver dollars to buttons he'd traced the gang to their hidey-hole. If they were on the lookout for visitors, it was a safe bet, too, that wouldn't be for laying on a welcome befitting a social caller.

At Joshua's distance, he could make out no sounds of life within the cabin. All that broke the gathering dusk was the inter-mittent, lonely cry of a mocking-bird. But Joshua didn't think his quarry could be any place else.

He peered round for signs of a guard to this robbers' roost.

'Yeah, mister, I'm right here,' said a guttural voice. 'So yuh kin hold it just where y'are!'

Joshua turned without haste, keeping his right hand visibly clear of his Colt. 'Hell, a sentry up a goddamn tree!' he muttered under this breath, despising himself for being suckered so promptly.

The watching owlhooter's vantage point was high in a majestic pine, the biggest around, free of limbs for some twenty feet from the ground. What Joshua should have seen was the knotted rope that dangled down the rough-barked trunk and which the sentry used to brace himself while he 'walked' down, the smooth stock of a shotgun tucked in the crook of his arm, his finger crooked round the trigger.

'Hoist 'em, stranger!' he growled. 'The boys ain't partial to snoopers.'

Joshua did as he was told. He had no choice. A blast from the Greener could rip him apart. And if it didn't, its ghastly racket would alert the stickup trio presumably holed up with others in the cabin. They would come running and he'd be trapped between the two seats of gunfire.

To grab any chance that might arise at all, he had to keep this one on one. A shout of alarm or the sound of an altercation was all it needed to bring out the others and tip the odds into impossible.

The sentry was an unshaven lout with blackened teeth and stinking breath. He shoved the shotgun right into Joshua's belly as he grinningly wrenched the Colt .45 out of the intruder's holster.

'What is all this?' Joshua mumbled vacantly, playing the innocent.

'Thet's what yuh's gonna tell us!' the sentry snarled. 'Yore pan is a new 'un on me, feller, but I gotta feelin' the boys kin put a name t' yore game!'

He prodded Joshua again with the shotgun. 'Git on down t' the camp, willya?'

Tension tautening every whipcord muscle in his body, Joshua took a step forward, trying to gauge how he should react to put his captor off his guard, knowing the jig would be up as soon as he was confronted by the others.

'Wal, I dunno – this ain't what I'd call friendly, it being a free country an' a man an American citizen an' all,' he said, feigning docility. 'Hell, that Greener o' your'n is enough to make a feller shiver his pants right off if they wasn't held up!'

'Quiet, smart ass! Or I'll blast yore guts t' dogs' meat!'

Joshua made a few more wobbly steps, striving to fool the sentry he was shaking in his boots. 'Jeez, you got me scared to death…'

He looked back over his shoulder, fixing wide eyes on the shotgun. Seemingly accidentally, he weaved off the indistinct path and into the loose shale that littered the slope down to the camp. Then all at once he went into a slip and crashed clumsily onto his backside.

For a few heart-stopping seconds he half-expected to feel the shot rip bloodily into his flesh. But the desperate gamble worked.

The outlaw laughed harshly at his awkward and apparently bone-jarring tumble, taking pleasure in Joshua's humiliation and his own ego-boosting power that had been its cause. He had this poor bastard at his mercy!

He jabbed him yet again in the ribs with the shotgun barrel.

'Git up, yuh blasted yeller-belly!'

That was when Joshua went into action – fast.

He clamped his hands around the gun barrel with a grip as powerful as a vice. Simultaneously, he thrust his body sideways out from under its black muzzle and planted his upflung right boot forcefully into the outlaw's groin.

The man came hurtling forward over Joshua's head in unavoidable response to a vicious wrench. He let the shotgun slither from his hold. The white-hot pain that knifed through his vitals paralysed every nerve in his body. He failed even to crook his trigger finger and the weapon clattered off down the slope, unfired. Which was what Joshua wanted in this fight – no guns, no noise.

Joshua was up and astride his opponent before he could recover.

He lammed a punch into the wretch's

white face. But the man wasn't finished yet. With the strength of a murderous rage, he heaved himself up, arching his body. That and the swing of his punch rocked Joshua off balance.

Joshua toppled and the pair rolled in a mess of flailing fists through the scrub.

Whether by chance or intent, a ferocious punch from the outlaw caught Joshua full on the nape of the neck. It was a punch of the cruellest kind – a rabbit punch that seemed to Joshua to come close to snapping the top of his spine. It made his head spin and his sight swim just as they came up against a large boulder.

His opponent tore free with a grunt of satisfaction. He slammed a great open right hand at Joshua's face. It crashed the outlaw-hunter's head against the boulder, and the thick, nail-bitten fingers splayed and groped fiendishly for Joshua's eye sockets.

'I'm gonna kill yuh!' the outlaw gasped out, his filthy breath coming in great pants.

Joshua knew he had to get the upper hand

and silence the enraged man before he found the sense and strength of voice to summon his pards.

Pushing against the boulder with his legs and arms, he heaved forward bodily. The outlaw was thrust back like a herded bull and tripped on his own high boot heels. But as he lost his footing he remembered Joshua's purloined Colt stuck in the waistband of his pants.

Joshua saw the drop of the outlaw's hand for the gun butt and instantly swung his right foot in a swift kick. His hard toe struck the hardcase's forearm just above the wrist.

The Colt roared, its snout spewing red flame, the slug going skywards. It was the first and only shot, because Joshua's savage kick hurled the gun from the outlaw's grasp.

But it was enough to do the damage to Joshua's chances even if it immediately saved his life.

The outlaw dived to retrieve the revolver and Joshua went after him, knowing the fight was won and lost at the same time.

Behind him he heard the cabin disgorging its occupants. Footsteps clattered urgently, and voices were raised in consternation.

Joshua was still trading punishing punches with the erstwhile sentry when rough hands seized him and he was hauled off.

Resistance was futile. Two of the newcomers flung him to the ground and jerked his arms behind his back and pinioned his wrists with a leather thong.

'By God!' said Butch Simich, snorting down his beaky nose. 'I swear it's the same sonofabitch thet braced us on the Tucson trail!'

'Finish 'im, Butch!' the winded fighter spluttered through the blood pumping from his split lips. 'I caught the bastard sneakin' up on us!'

But Simich's wrath had cooled. There was plenty about this he didn't understand. It was supposed to have been an easy job. His sponsors had assured him of it. Simich knew his place in the scheme of things, and it wasn't bucking big boys. The Wells Fargo haul would have been riches beyond belief. Yet it was the kind of loot he couldn't have disposed of himself, and he'd been relying on others whose information had already let him down.

Was treachery afoot? This dangerous-looking hombre was a professional fighting man, sure thing. A Wells Fargo agent maybe? If so, others might come sniffing around, like nosey hounds, and it would be time he and his boys quit their comforts in this neck of the woods and headed for quieter pastures.

'Naw, Lafe,' he rasped. 'I wanna know how we stands. It could be a hun'erd times worse 'n looks. Mebbe some louse is playin' us fer the world's biggest suckers an' aimin' to put rope neckties around our gizzards! This gent is gonna do some singin' fer us, I figger. He cashes in his chips when I says so.'

Lafe sneered. 'Whatever yuh says, boss.'

He turned and spat out a chilling promise, his blood-flecked spittle spraying over Joshua like venom. 'But I'm gonna be makin' the snaky cuss wish he *was* dead long before he steps off!'

Joshua jerked his head back, riding the blow, as Lafe slammed a hard-bunched fist into his unprotected face. Even so, his cheek throbbed with pain and his eyes were left glistening.

'Talk, skunk!' Simich demanded. 'Damn yuh, who put yuh up t' this?'

7

Water of Death

Dorothy-May stormed into the kitchen at the Pennydale Ford stage station and crashed down the used mugs, plates and pots she'd collected up in the dining-room.

Ezra Pennydale parted his lips from the neck of a bottle and winced. 'Hell's bells, daughter!' he complained with a belly-shaking belch. 'Thet din's done busted m' head!'

'Huh! 'T ain't my doin' if yore head's a-ringin'. More like thet rotten redeye!'

'None o' yore lip, child! I bin drinkin' this here stuff since afore yuh was even a seed – an' it ain't never done me no harm neither!' He belched again and hiccupped.

'You'se sore 'cos thet fancy gent put yore nose outa joint,' he added with wisdom.

'Horse droppin's!' Dorothy-May shot back fierily. 'I don't pay no mind to what greenhorn passengers says!'

Old Ezra closed his watery eyes and shook his sizzled head, clearing the fumes.

'I hear'd nuff o' your confab. An' it shore sounded diff'rent t' me. He up an' says–' here Ezra assumed a judge's dignity, 'an' I quotes – "Yuh kin git a man hanged blabbin' mischief like thet around, Miss Pennydale!" An' yuh says, huffy-like, "I won't never waste my dimes on yore novels ag'in."'

Ezra broke off in a peal of cackling laughter, whether at his performance as a mimic of an affronted New York City gentleman or at Dorothy-May's reddening face, was untellable.

For the forthright girl, it was nearly all too much, straining the ties of blood and threatening to curtail the ever-shaky maintenance of filial respect for her drunken, lazybones parent.

How any woman could ever have let her be born to this decrepit critter when he was already in his forties and admittedly set in his self-indulgent ways, Dorothy-May had long ago ceased to wonder. The poor woman herself had died when she was but an infant and too young to enquire.

What was especially galling at this present time was that the ornery old man had got it all off right. A deplorable but inescapable rift had deepened between herself and the illustrious Clement P. Conway, writer, over her plainly expressed opinions of Marshal Virgil Lyons.

Clem had been determined to cast the man he called the 'Lion of the Law' as a frontier hero. He'd travelled all those weary miles in railroad cars and jolting stage-coaches just to do it! He avowed he was going to interview Lyons and glorify him in his next orange-covered epic.

The very thought of the unworthy badge-packer being so immortalised made Dorothy-May go hot all over again. How could she save Clem, and his unsuspecting audience, from such misplaced hero-worship?

She remembered being told by an itinerant merchant that dime novels had a huge sale; Edward S. Ellis' *Seth Jones: or The Captives of the Frontier* had actually sold more than four thousand copies! The enormity of such fame awaiting old Lyons was intolerable.

Dorothy-May threw cutlery into a drawer with unnecessary force, ignoring Ezra's renewed protests. 'Lyons is a fake – an' what's worse he's in cahoots with thet slimy, underhanded rattlesnake of a saloon-keeper!' she scolded. 'What's a gal t' do?'

She bustled through the remaining station chores, her mind already made up whether she knew it or not. Clem had left in the company of Marshal Lyons and Sanders' wife, Lucia Marques, for Hellyer's Creek, some time ago. But they would not be setting a fast pace and she could ride after them.

'Thet pore li'le innocent man needs protectin' from wicked Western ways,' she reasoned. 'By crackity! His head were scraped by a bullet! 'T ain't no wonder his reasonin's gone wrong...'

Ezra smiled maliciously, baring his broken teeth. 'Shore yuh ain't gotten sorta sweet on the feller?' he probed.

Dorothy-May scoffed. 'Men! I ain't got no time for 'em. All the spec'mens I sees is ornery, two-timin', bone-idle, low-down rats! Ain't no *real* man ever set foot aroun' Hell'er's Crik! Howsomever, I figger it's like I says. A blind man c'd see Mr Conway needs proper directin'.'

There was more soliloquising, muttered and mental, along these lines, so that eventually Dorothy-May was convinced she would, for shame, be failing in hospitality and public duty not to saddle up and set off *pronto* in the tracks of her fallen literary idol.

Old Ezra shook his grizzled head and broached another bottle when his turbulent child rode out purposefully on a fresh horse and set it loping down the trail toward Hellyer's Creek.

'Goddamnit, the gal's plumb loco agoin' chasin' after a soft-handed pen-pusher! Jest when she shoulda bin gittin' some chow cookin' … it's a whiles since I et.'

He cussed disgustedly. 'Too blasted impulsive! Nuff t' drive a father t' immoderate drink!'

Dorothy-May didn't know what she was going to say when she caught up with Lyons' party, but she'd already been drawn into the game anyway, and her hand wasn't played out yet.

Her course decided and her motives rationalised, Dorothy-May wasn't ducking out nohow!

She took a seldom-used cut-off trail which intercepted the stage road again some several miles from the way station. Coming back onto the road, she saw the little knot of riders stirring the dust ahead.

Of the three, Marshal Virgil Lyons was the least happy for the party to be joined by the girl from Pennydale Ford.

Lucia Marques regarded a dusty journey on horseback as the greatest trial in itself.

Totally unbecoming for a lady of her background and talents, darling.

Clem Conway, beginning to appreciate he'd been dumped in the midst of a real-life adventure, was manfully ignoring his throbbing head. The row with this girl who'd so boldly assisted them, and was now solicitously rejoining them, he would write off to misunderstanding and her lack of education and finesse. Thus he would prove that even in great adversity and under much provocation, his chivalry had not been exhausted.

But Virgil Lyons wore grim worry furrows between his bushy white brows. This red-headed kid of old Pennydale's was a damn' nuisance. There was the hombre Dillard, for sure. Yet he figured it was largely Dorothy-May's stepping-in over the stage stickup that had tipped the fat into the fire as far as he was concerned. The interfering, pants-wearing female! Ezra should have gotten her into line with a quirt long ago, except he was always too busy with a bottle.

Lyons did not look forward to the inevitable upset the botched stickup was going to cause with Lucia's husband, Dice Sanders.

And what had Lucia been doing on the stage? He could only guess, but he had a mighty good idea what kind of effect it would have had on the raiders.

Women! They should be kept strictly in kitchens and the upstairs rooms of saloons. But it was not to be. Here was this carrot-headed one now, chirping away like a jaybird.

'Hey, look, Mr Conway!' Dorothy-May said, pointing to the side of a hill, where a house had been built, part dugout and part earthen bricks. 'Thar's the soddy I was tellin' yuh about. An' see thet bale o' cheese-cloth hidden 'mongst those ol' nail kegs an' soap boxes?'

The pair were riding stirrup to stirrup. Clem could just see a corner of loose-woven fabric flapping in the breeze. Even had he been looking for it, he would have been hard put to spot it. Dorothy-May's eyes were as sharp as her wits and her tongue.

'Thet was stolen from a consignment off-loaded for holdin' over at the way station.'

Virgil Lyons broke in with a vigorous protest. 'Now watch your mouth, Miss Pennydale! Thet's an unsubstantiated accusation, y'unnerstand, an' yuh got no right to tell stranger folk suchlike.'

'What'd I say?' Dorothy-May muttered to Clem. 'Puffed-up ol' turkey cock!'

''Sides,' went on the marshal, 'what would them poor Mexes be doin' with cheese-cloth? Prob'ly given 'em as throw-outs they can't use anyhows.'

'Hog's ass! They used most all o' it – strung up under the rafters fer roof linin',' the girl proclaimed with knowledgeable triumph. She turned back confidingly to Clem. 'Dirt an' grass fall like raindrops inside them soddies,' she explained.

On rounding the corner of the long, low house, there came into a view a neat spring buggy. A well-groomed, hammer-headed grey was between the shafts.

'Marshal Lyons! D'yuh see who it is?' the

girl cried, hauling on the reins and drawing her mount to a stop. 'Thet's Doc McBride's rig!'

'So it is, gal,' Lyons said sourly. 'Even squatter folk's entitled to call the sawbones, I guess, though I doubt they kin pay.'

'We gotta stop fer Mr Conway here. The doc kin check his head wound pr'fessionally right off, 'stead o' trailin' on inta town when he ain't gonna be thar.'

'Makes sense, I guess,' Lyons conceded gruffly.

Lucia clucked her tongue, irritated at the thought of more delay, and Clem was embarrassed at being made the centre of attention.

'No, no,' the New Yorker protested. 'I'll be quite all right, I assure you. You've dressed the wound nicely, thank you, Miss Pennydale.'

'Aw, c'mon, Mr Conway,' she said, setting her chin determinedly. 'It won't take more'n a coupla shakes.'

'Well, perhaps,' he said meekly. 'Look isn't

that a well over there? Couldn't we stop for a quick drink, and if the doctor comes out while we're there, all well and good.'

The compromise sounded dandy to Dorothy-May, while Lyons just grumped into his tobacco-stained moustache and Lucia sighed gustily at being so continuously upstaged.

They'd just dismounted and Dorothy-May was figuring out the mechanics of the rope and iron-hooped wooden pail when a gaunt little man wearing a black frock coat hurtled out of the house through a door crudely screened by a tatty buffalo hide.

Clem gaped as the man rushed toward them on spindly legs at a speed that threatened to trip him up.

'Stop! Stop!' the man screeched.

'Why, Doctor McBride! Whatever's the matter?' Lucia asked, her painted lashes fluttering wide.

The medico pushed past her and straight up to Dorothy-May.

'Young lady, drop that pail back this

moment!' he snapped breathlessly.

The little man's distressful agitation impressed even the independently-minded Dorothy-May. She let the pail fall with an echoing splash.

'We weren't *stealin'* nothin', doc,' she said. 'Jest helpin' us-selfs t' a li'le drink.'

'Drink that water and ye'll drink with the devil himself!' he stated. 'That's all.'

The marshal drew himself up, throwing out his tin-starred chest. 'Howdy, doc. Mebbeso yuh'd care to inform us what's bothering yuh.'

'Yessir!' McBride clipped. 'This here well is poison, I tell ye.' He nodded toward the sod house, where a woman wailed. 'The cholera is here. I can do nothing for Pedro Alvarez. He'll be ready for burial by morn', and two of his bairns are already gone.'

McBride was an enlightened practitioner for his times, who prided himself on his work, be it dependent on unorthodox folk cures or knowledge from well-bound textbooks that gave no allowances for the frontier condition He paid much attention to the lessons of experience and observation.

'The cholera is food-borne and water-borne,' he maintained to his shocked listeners. 'I fear poor sanitation has allowed it to contaminate the very necessity of life whose availability drew these people here. The water in this well can no longer be assumed fit to drink. Do so and ye'll almost certainly die. In the morn ye'll be in the throes of abdominal spasms. By even yorr body will be a dry husk, emptied by constant watery discharges. Prostration and death will quickly follow.'

Lyons visibly wilted at the feisty sawbones' vivid account of an infected victim's fate. 'Much obliged t' yuh, doc. Sounds a whole heap worse 'n snakebite. Let's get outa the place, folks!'

And that was what they did, the marshal spurring his horse on like the bacteria was pursuing him hotfoot down the trail.

Dorothy-May took the opportunity to re turn to her putting-down of the veteran star-toter. 'By crackity! This hyar choly-ra has shore put the wind up ol' Lyons' tail,' she said to Clem. 'Ain't never seen 'im move so fast since th' hornets' nest got busted outside his office winder!'

Clem wondered what her intentions were in following the party. Was it just his masculine vanity to suppose she might be interested in *him?* But if so, why was she going out of her way to rub his fur up the wrong way, so to speak? She knew he had nothing but admiration for the venerable 'Lion of the Law'.

He admired the girl, too, of course. Her flight from the outlaw gang had been plucky indeed. Her selfless, frantic ride out for reinforcements had proved the turning-point in a dire struggle.

It was a great pity she was obsessed with this irrational distrust and dislike of the old marshal. Maybe it was the fault of her wreck of a father that she evidenced such lack of respect for her elders, Clem's muzzy thoughts ran, unconsciously trying to absolve her of blame. Ezra Pennydale was clearly an old soak, just as Lucia had warned, and treated Dorothy-May as his drudge. But was that an excuse for her malicious tale-telling?

Lucia made a bid for Clem's distracted attention.

'To think we might have drunk water from a poisoned well!' she wailed. 'I declare it makes cold shudders go down my spine.'

'Well, ma'am, you mustn't let it bother you now. The doctor was there and in time to save us. Fate is still on our side, I guess.'

'Do you think that, Mr Conway? I so hope you're right. It's been such a terrible day. Us theatre folk are sensitive souls, y'know. We feel the vibrations from other planes, darling. And I do believe it isn't over yet. When we reach Hellyer's Creek, I fear something perfectly dreadful is going to happen...'

8

A Woman's Fury

Hellyer's Creek was shaking itself out of *siesta* mode; the hot sun was westering and the greater part of the day was done. At the Silver Buckle, an out-of-tune piano tinkled tinny notes of tawdry invitation and a drone of uncouth conversation within announced that some had taken it up.

The town was built at the junction of two sluggish streams that in their united state flowed on to drain ultimately into the Gila River.

Its founding fathers, if land speculators and entrepreneurs could be called that, had entertained high hopes for Hellyer's Creek, based on cattle and mining. Spaniards had introduced cattle into the country in the early seventeenth century; likewise, the first silver discoveries had been Spanish. There was gold, too, while copper – said the industrialists back East – would one day overshadow them all.

But meanwhile the founders' hopes had not been realised, not even with the cattle and the silver, and their particular township was a dead-end place, shunned by all except the flotsam unable for one reason or another to carve out more prosperous lives in other, demonstrably thriving communities.

It was the kind of unlovely place where law-abiding men even chewed their tobacco in slow motion, because there wasn't much honest to do when you'd finished that. The wide, sandy Main Street was flanked by the usual two rows of false fronts, distinguished in this case only by a more-than-average peeling of sun-blistered paint. On the street were several stores, a smithy, livery barn, bank, marshal's office, stage station and hotel. And, of course, the garish Silver Buckle.

Arriving in the town, the marshal's party split up and went separate ways: Lyons headed for his office, Lucia for the impressive house behind the Silver Buckle, and Clem, accompanied by Dorothy-May, for the hotel.

'As a witness I'll report to your office with a full, written account of the stage murders as soon as I'm able,' Clem promised Lyons as they parted.

'Oh… Ah, yeah – you do that, Mr Conway,' said Lyons, not with any enthusiasm.

'And later, when you're less busy, of course, I hope you'll grant me the inestimable favour of letting me record for print some reminiscences of your outstanding career.'

Dorothy-May quietly fumed. The poor fish was bowing and scraping to the twisting has-been like he was a little tin god!

After the pair had moved off, Lyons unlocked his office and went in. He threw his hat onto the antlers above the scarred rosewood desk and slumped weakly into the creaking chair behind before fumbling a bottle out of the bottom drawer.

A previous occupant of the dingy little office, having a missionary turn of mind, had left a framed text yellowing on the facing wall. It proclaimed, 'Resist the devil, and he will flee from you.'

Lyons ruminated that where matters spiritual were concerned, old man Pennydale might have the immediate and surer solution for ageing sinners like himself. He tipped the redeye straight down his gizzard from the bottle.

It was a sad and shaming pass he was brought to, administering the crooked law in a one-horse, no-account place like this. But a man couldn't feed and clothe himself on reputation and past glories. Younger, more able officers had succeeded him in brighter burgs – men with hard eyes and fast reflexes; men just like that Dillard fellow who'd dared to go up against him today.

It was something he bitterly resented. He'd show them yet though.

Rejection and demotion had tapped a dark spring in his nature and it was set to bubble to the top. He was still a dangerous man to buck – forked lightning with a gun, no bragging – and he'd cling to Dice Sanders' coat-tails long enough to collect his dues...

Why, if things had panned out like they'd supposed to, like Sanders had said, he'd be a rich man right now, instead of sitting here sinking the comfort of his last bottle.

And nursing a strange feeling that before long all hell was going to be let loose in Hellyer's Creek.

Lucia Marques had reached the gate in the trim white picket fence around the handsome Sanders residence before she remembered she was returning home from Tucson empty-handed. All the little luxuries she'd procured there were still out on the stage road, in the trunk roped to the roof of the wrecked coach. Damn, she thought, the expedition had been in vain!

No, that wasn't entirely correct. She'd had

another purpose, hadn't she? And that was to make this unexpected return a day early, so that she might check up on how her spouse conducted himself in her absence.

She wouldn't put anything past some of the brazen hussies Dice had working for him at the Silver Buckle, and men being men...

Dice was probably over at the saloon now, ostensibly to mingle with his customers. But she would need to change her dusty clothes and freshen up before she surprised him – and anyone who might be with him – in his backroom office.

It was her own home, but the small deceit she was practicing in returning unannounced, plus maybe feminine intuition, prompted her to act cautiously. She slid the key into the brass lock of the polished oak door with the stealth of a thief and turned it slowly lest the levers in the mechanism should click.

In the entrance hall she paused. A hint of strange perfume was on the air. Her narrowed eyes travelled up the balustraded stairs. Surely that was light spilling onto the top landing from one of the bedrooms. But it was barely dusk. Who would have been here to light a kerosene lamp at this hour?

Then she heard a mumble of voices and a low chuckle.

'Who's there?' she called out, her vague suspicions taking on such sudden and solid validity that she was startled.

Dice was not only dallying with one of his painted whores – he'd had the effrontery to bring her back to the house. Their home!

From upstairs she heard a cry, broken off as though by a muffling hand; a creak of springs and a rustling and scrambling.

Lifting her ruffled skirt, Lucia sped up the stairs. The door to the main bedroom was ajar and the knob was snatched from her hand as she went to enter.

Dice Sanders stood in the doorway, dressed in a blue silk robe, picking his teeth with an air of calm, his pudgy fingers unshaking, though sweat beaded his white brow.

'Lucia, by all that's holy!' he began suavely.

'Stand back, you disgusting louse, and let me in!' Lucia raged.

'Why, whatever's the matter, dear?' He continued blocking the way with his paunchy bulk, his obsidian eyes unwavering and an icy smirk on his wet lips.

'Stand back, I say, or so help me I'll jab your eyes out!' She whipped a long and wicked pin from her hat.

He took an exasperated breath, blowing out his bloated cheeks resignedly. 'If you insist, Lucia, but I can't think what's come over you.'

She swept into the room, taking in its apparent emptiness and the rumpled bed-sheets in her first swift glance.

'What have you done with her?'

'Done with whom, my precious?'

'Don't come the innocent with me, Daniel Sanders! You've had a woman in here, I know it!' Her voice was crackling with anger.

Sanders shrugged his silk-clad shoulders with resignation. 'A ridiculous accusation!'

He laughed, showing his gold-filled teeth. 'Why, you can see for yourself, I was alone in the room.'

She watched him, contempt and hatred smouldering within her. 'In bed at this hour?' she asked scathingly.

'Sure. I gotta headache as a matter of fact.'

His bland self-assurance infuriated her. She prowled around the room, her bosom heaving, trying to master her temper, looking about her.

The floor-length drapes that concealed the balcony window stirred. Was it just the disturbance made by her passage?

She made a lunge and swept the heavy red folds aside.

'Come out, you little cow!'

The bleach-blonde called Cora screamed, and it was all on.

Lucia grabbed Cora and dragged her in from the balcony.

Cora squirmed and shrieked. Her thigh-length white shift rode up and the hatpin punctured the most bounteously rounded portion of her anatomy.

'*Eek!*' she screeched.

The bloodstained hatpin slipped from Lucia's grip, but she yanked at the long tresses of Cora's straw-coloured hair and threw her to the floor, in a flurry of threshing white limbs.

'You dirty yowling bitch! Your wares won't be fit for sale when I've finished with them!'

She kicked a hard toe of her patent-leather footwear into the saloon girl's soft right breast where it spilled loosely over the plunging neckline of the disarranged shift.

'Dice! Dice! Save me!' the terrified jade wailed. She started to struggle to her feet, clutching her painful breast, and Lucia waded into her, slapping her cheeks alternately with stinging, open-handed blows.

Sanders was by nature a man who dodged physical confrontation wherever possible, but he saw he had to intervene before murder was done.

'Stop that, you stupid hell-cat!' he burst out, trying to insinuate his not inconsiderable bulk between the two struggling, sobbing women.

Putting his beringed fingers under his wife's chin, he pulled her head back.

She gave a quick jerk of her head and instantly buried her teeth in the back of his hand.

He howled in agony and tore his hand away, while Cora, taking advantage of the diversion of Lucia's ferocity, ripped herself free from Lucia's clutching hands and fled from the room in the tatters of her shift.

Cheated of revenge on the hapless woman, and having lost the vicious pin, Lucia snatched up a hand-mirror, ornately framed in gilt, from the dressing-table. With it, she rained heavy blows on her cowering husband's head, spitting out forgotten obscenities in languages she'd not used for years.

The mirror shattered. Blood flowed.

'Mercy, woman, mercy!' he cried hoarsely.

If he hadn't really had a headache before, he had one now. His head swam like he'd been on a bender.

Outside the house Cora, scuttling in her near-nakedness for the back way into the saloon, wondered whether murder was still to be done, if not her own.

But Sanders at last made the bedroom door and stumbled out and onto the stairs. He immediately fell down them, as surely as though he'd put his soft, flabby foot on a wet cake of soap. He rolled into a robe-tangled heap of bruised flesh at the bottom.

Not waiting to see if his wife would follow, he leapt to his feet with alacrity and scuttled through the open main door and across the dusty alley to the Silver Buckle.

Lucia's wrath had spent every last vestige of an energy already depleted by stickups and gunfights and trail riding. She slammed the bedroom door behind her unfaithful partner and stood back against it, limp from exertion and gasping for breath.

'The beast,' she sobbed. 'The filthy rotten beast! He hasn't finished paying for this!'

'You're wasting your time,' Joshua Dillard repeated. 'I ain't telling you scum nothing!'

'Who are yuh an' how happen you was ridin' after the stage?' Butch Simich pressed.

'What the hell was yuh doin' sneakin' around our camp?' demanded Lafe.

'Jest doing my business,' Joshua said more coolly than he felt.

'Let's finish 'im off and lay 'im out fer the buzzards, Simich!' another owlhoot snapped curtly.

'Suit yourselfs,' Joshua shrugged. 'The jig's up anyways. Your next dance is gonna be on air!'

'How d'yuh mean?'

'I wasn't fool enough to follow you this far on my lonesome,' Joshua bluffed. 'There's a posse out there on your tails. You ain't gonna stickup a mail coach an' kill its crew an' not raise a helluva ruckus!'

'A real smart customer, ain't yuh?' jeered Simich, kicking him in the ribs. 'This posse outa Hell'er's Crik?'

'Mebbe.'

The gathered owlhoots grinned and sniggered.

'Hey, lissen, boys!' Simich jeered. 'This galoot reckons he's got ol' Lyons on the prod. I figger he don't know nothin'. He's all mouth. Why, he prob'ly don't even know what day o' the week it is!'

'Yuh all wet, mister,' Lafe said. His eyes were as expressionless as a striking rattlesnake's. 'An' I'm jest gonna punch yore face in ag'in!'

The foul-breathed owlhoot hauled Joshua to his feet by his shirtfront. He was balling his fist and Joshua was poised to receive a bone-smashing blow when the proceedings were interrupted by an excited cry from another of the gang from outside the cabin.

'I've found the polecat's cayuse!' he hollered.

The man came bursting in, a wild look of discovery on his face. He dumped an opened saddlebag on the dirty floor and plunged his hands amongst its rifled contents till he retrieved a bunch of crumpled papers.

'His handle's Joshua Dillard.'

'Dillard!' jerked Simich, scratching his beaky nose. 'Ain't he a *Pinkerton?*'

The detective agency was respected and feared through many States. A criminal knew that once his name was in its 'rogues' gallery,' the file wasn't closed until he was officially declared dead. Pinkerton agents had successfully infiltrated and scattered several notorious outlaw bands.

Lafe growled. 'Hell, I dunno. Weren't a Dillard pulled out up Chicago way? Sided with a workers' union or somesuch when the Pinkertons was workin' for their bosses.'

'Naw, it was later he quit,' said Simich, the strain of hard thinking twisting his face. 'This Dillard was the jasper whose wife was killed by the Wilder gang in Texas. I'd heard told someplace he dropped out...'

Lafe slapped Joshua's face. 'Yuh still workin' fer Pinkerton, feller? Or yuh on the Wells Fargo payroll or somep'n?'

Joshua grunted but said nothing.

Simich was in a dilemma. If this spy was a

lone wolf, they could fix him with no hassles. But if other agents were at hand, with the might of a nationwide organisation behind them, it mightn't be so easy.

'This mess ain't our makin',' he rasped. 'I ain't bein' hounded by no Pinkertons. I say we put the heat on the guys in Hell'er's Crik. If they ain't got the right answers, we're lightin' a shuck. We'll hotfoot fer the Border an' lie low among the greasers.'

Lafe snarled an oath. 'I volunteer t' ride inta town meself, boss. Mebbe this bastard jest had his own ideas about thet bank coin. If'n I git the word, I'm gonna be back to pull 'im to bits personal!'

9

The Marshal Sees Red

Marshal Lyons had imbibed the best part of his quart bottle of liquor of the unlabelled variety Dice Sanders allocated to those who rendered him services and favours.

Deep down it rankled that a cheap saloon owner and one-time gambler should not only be his benefactor, but that he should also have him in his gaudy vest pocket along with the rest of the drab little town. The vestiges of his pride made it hard for him to face the facts. Without Sanders' payoffs and influence, he'd probably be broke and out of a job.

He'd be in the poorhouse, or a hobo begging for his grub, a bed of straw, his clothes and baccy. The days of glory as the

Lion of the Law counted for nothing. The world was brat fickle.

Though it blurred his vision, the raw drink he'd swigged also let him see things more clearly and gave him a courage of sorts. So when Sanders came raging into his office, as he'd known he would, he was ready for him.

'Bin kinda expectin' yuh, Dice. I've bin put in a corner by this stagecoach mess, yuh know.'

The marshal's belligerence did nothing to soothe Sanders' ragged temper.

'Now see here!' he said angrily. 'What happens on the ground is your end of the operation. My part was procuring knowledge of that secret Wells Fargo shipment.'

'Huh! An' thet was easy. Fer a banker, Willie Fulcher's real stoopid. Fancy fallin' fer yore fixed roulette layouts! It was plain reckless to lose all them thousands, even without lettin' yuh pile up IOUs to hold over 'im.'

'I haven't come here to discuss my methods, Lyons,' Sanders responded hotly.

'Naw ... I reckon yuh ain't.'

It filtered through to the marshal that Sanders was far from his usual smooth self, even allowing for the failure of the scheme he'd masterminded to hit Wells, Fargo & Company for fifty thousand dollars.

'Say, Dice, you bin workin' out with one o' your own bouncers or summat?' He screwed up his eyes the better to see the bruises and splits that marred the gambler's visage. 'Them's mighty colourful injuries.'

'I haven't come here to discuss my appearance either!'

Lyons drew himself up.

'A marshal's got a right to ask, ain't he? Seems like he's got a job t' do if'n some hell-raiser's beatin' up prominent citizens.'

'If you must know, this is my dear wife's work.' Sanders scowled. 'She sneaked back from Tucson a day early and got unreasonable when she found I had company.'

Lyons nodded wisely. 'Oh, yeah ... Lucia was on the stage, weren't she?' He waggled the near-empty bottle. 'Mebbe thet was the problem, Dice.'

'What do you mean?' Sanders snapped.

'Wal, seems to me like it could of thrown Butch Simich an' his boys t' find Mrs Sanders ridin' the stage. Spesh'ly when they bin told thar weren't no passengers.'

'I was misinformed ... they were unexpected, last-minute bookings,' Sanders blustered. 'Simich could've gone ahead and killed Lucia for all I care!'

Lyons' shaggy white brows rose. 'But Butch weren't to know thet, hey? He'd of figgered it would of put a spoke in the wheel to kill the big man's wife!'

Sanders reflected bitterly it was amazing how alcohol had sharpened this old idiot's wits and bolstered his insolent nerve.

'Are you blaming me, Lyons, damn you?'

'Hell, no,' Lyons said sardonically. 'But if it weren't fer yore tomcattin' with the short-skirted charmers an' givin' Lucia suspicions, it might of worked out like it was meant to. Now I gotta do somethin' or hev this goddamn Dillard feller on m' neck! Yuh heard 'bout thet?'

'At the Buckle they aren't talking about anything except the stage stickup.' Sanders strode another length of the dingy office, fuming.

'We gotta put it t' rights, Dice. Set down, willya, an' stop leapin' about like a cat on hot bricks.'

'Don't give me orders, you old goat.'

'Now let's not git t' tradin' cuss words, pard'ner,' jeered Lyons. 'This job was goin' to set us up in clover for life, with yuh channelin' the proceeds through the gamin' tables an' across the bar at the saloon. An' I was set to quit with my share – shake off the dust o' this dump, remember?'

Sanders saw something out the window and smiled, his agile brain working fast. 'Sure. I've gotten to thinking I've had a bellyful of the place myself. It's time I ditched that squawking woman of mine and headed for lusher pastures.'

'I'd jest like to see yuh do thet with all yore *dinero* sunk in the Crik's Main Street an' the fifty thou' gone down the river.'

'Listen, Lyons, we ain't lost that loot yet. Sanders' little hog's eyes were hard and bright.

'How'd yuh figger thet?'

'That's what you and me are going to talk over next.'

Lyons saw the smugness creeping back into the saloon man's scratched and mauled face. What crazy damn scheme can he be hatching now, he wondered.

'Willie Fulcher's going to make one last gamble on clearing his debts,' Sanders purred. 'He'll play ball in the biggest game of his life! Your men have brought the money into his bank, right?'

Lyons nodded his white-maned head but looked puzzled.

'Well, Simich's sidekick Lafe Teed has ridden in. I've just seen his mean and dirty face. The gang probably wants to know what the hell's going on.'

Lyons looked morose. 'No doubtin' it, I'd say.'

'Then this is what you're going to tell them: They're robbing the bank tomorrow!'

Clem Conway tossed restlessly on his hotel bed. Doc McBride had been and gone, re-dressing his grazed head and exhorting him to take things easy for a day or two. But it was very hard even to contemplate following such obviously sound advice.

His mind would not unwind from the day's excitement and here he was at his des-tination – a dusty frontier town which to him seemed full of atmosphere, the promise of adventure and the romance of the fron-tier wilderness.

The room was simple, but seemed basic-ally clean and adequate. Besides the bed, it offered two straight-backed chairs with seat cushions covered in faded plush, a stand for hanging clothes, plus a commode with wash bowl and filled water pitcher, above which hung a brown-spotted mirror with a crack across one corner.

All acceptable enough. But through the

open window snatches of conversation floated up from the street below. And every other bated-breath word seemed to be 'stage' or 'stickup' or 'owlhoots'.

Eventually, Clem made up his mind. It was no good – he'd have to defy the sawbones' well-meant edict and venture out. He was sure Marshal Virgil Lyons would not deny him the latest news of the raid on the stage. Why, at this moment an intense manhunt might be in operation. Maybe the man Dillard would have already tracked the outlaws to their lair and reported in to the veteran lawman, who would know just what to do.

It would be good, too, to speak to the Lion of the Law without having to worry about the girl from the Pennydale Ford stage station. Dorothy-May was a brave and admirable person in many ways, of course, but with a rural simplicity and the silliness of immaturity warping her judgement where a respected member of the old generation was concerned. Clem had found her succinct commentaries embarrassing.

He dressed and left the room. Clutching his now travel-battered derby, he went along the short, musty-smelling corridor, dimly lit by oil lamps turned low, and descended a flight of threadbare-carpeted stairs to the lobby.

The bald-headed clerk who'd earlier got him to sign the register and allocated his room dropped his newspaper with a surprised exclamation and rushed out from behind his desk. He narrowly missed upsetting a dusty-looking pot plant.

'Mr Conway! Is everything all right, sir?'

'Certainly. I decided I needed some air.'

The clerk frowned. 'The doctor told me I was to supply all your needs to your room for two days.'

'He was being over-cautious, but I won't be going far. I'll probably just step across to the marshal's office and back, that's all.'

Clem made a rapid exit, fearing the officious clerk might try to restrain him.

It was already getting dark outside. Pitch

pine torches were stuck in metal brackets at the corners where various dark side alleys gave onto Main Street.

Most of the activity centred around the saloon. Horses stood flank to flank at the hitching rack. Large letters on the ornate frontage advertised its business, but the signage was scarcely necessary – its brightness and noise, compounded of piano music and liquor-loosened tongues, made it impossible to miss.

Clem passed it by and clumped into the shadows of the awning-shaded boardwalk that fronted a block of smaller establishments including the marshal's office.

A thick paper blind had been drawn down over the office's window, but chinks of lamplight shafted out around it, showing the place was occupied. He was about to rap on the door, when something about the contentious tone of the voices from within gave him pause.

Was Marshal Lyons dealing with a troublemaker?

Clem didn't want to butt in on what was none of his business, but he was essentially a person of an inquisitive frame of mind. He couldn't help himself. He glanced swiftly right and left along the darkened boardwalk then put his hand to the doorknob. It turned easily and the door gave to his stealthy pressure, opening the narrowest of cracks.

Every word now came clearly to his ears.

'Stickin' up the stage out on the trail was one thing,' said the marshal's voice. 'But turnin' a blind eye to a bank robbery right here under m' nose in m' own town is somep'n else!'

'Don't be such a weak-kneed old fool, Lyons! It's a cracker of a proposition. What will it matter what folks think? We ain't gonna be sticking around.'

'Wal, I dunno, Dice. It sounds kinda risky...'

'Risky, my ass! You're the law here, ain't you? Who's to go against us? Banker Fulcher will be forced to co-operate, I'll fix that, and the lily-livered townsfolk will duck for cover to a man. You and me'll ride out with the Simich gang and the money … all we can put in a wagon!'

Clem stood rooted to the spot, momentarily paralysed by the damning nature of what his innocent eavesdropping had turned up.

'All right, Dice,' the marshal said. 'It don't look like I got a lotta options. Thet Dillard hombre worries me a mite though. I s'pose he'll hit town afore tomorrer an' be right here when it all happens. Prob'ly be hasslin' me to git out after Simich an' his bunch at a guess.'

'To hell with range dicks, if that's what he is! You ain't lost your *nerve*, have you, Lyons?'

'Nope. But I smells trouble.'

Clem heard the ominous click of a six-gun's hammer thumbed back and the spin of the cylinder.

'Don't fool around with that thing, Lyons! You've been drinking.'

'Hah! Who's nervy now, eh? Gotta practice

m' draw, ain't I? Fast as ever, see? An' a li'le liquor jest steadies the ol' hand.'

A chair scraped on bare floorboards as it was hurriedly pushed back. 'Tomorrow then. You fix the details with Teed, then get back to me so I can square the rest with Willie Fulcher.'

Clem took to his heels. He'd heard more than enough and hanging around would lead to his discovery.

He retraced his steps to the hotel, appalled at the evidence of his own ears.

'Holy cow! The Lion of the Law under the thumb of a crooked saloon-keeper!' Clem muttered his disbelief to himself.

But he could have made no mistake. What he'd overheard had been proof that a conspiracy was being laid to rob the bank with the marshal's connivance!

His next problem was that he had a moral duty as a law-abiding citizen to do something – and fast – about what was being planned. He had to report the matter to higher authorities, maybe in Tucson or at

Fort Yuma, if the imminent robbery of the bank was to be thwarted.

But whom could he turn to? The only law on the scene was corrupt. Joshua Dillard came to mind as the most capable and obvious alternative. After all, he was apparently some kind of law enforcer and had demonstrated his interest after the stage stickup. The way he'd turned up couldn't have been coincidence. But the man had vanished on the trail of the outlaw gang and hadn't yet shown in town. Maybe he'd already come to some grief himself! He'd taken on heavy odds, that was for certain.

A wire? Certainly there was a telegraph office at the stage station. But Clem had a shrewd suspicion that like everything else in Hellyer's Creek it would be under the ultimate control of Dice Sanders or his tame lawdog. If he blew any whistles that way, he'd only put himself in danger and to no avail.

Besides, who would take any notice of him? He had no official standing whatsoever.

If the message got where it was supposed to – and telegrams in these primitive parts frequently went by roundabout routes – it would probably be pigeonholed and investigated sometime never.

Fighting men were needed on the spot. And they would have to begin riding immediately if they were to arrive by tomorrow.

There was no one he could turn to, Clem concluded, feeling desperately helpless. Then, with just a faint glimmer of hope, he thought of Dorothy-May Pennydale. Maybe she'd know what could be done.

10

Dillard's Trick

Joshua Dillard was tied hand and foot. As well as the leather thong at his wrists, his ankles had been roped. More cords held his upper arms to his body. Simich was taking no chances. Only a knife could get him out of the bonds.

He was bundled into one of the shacks at the owlhoots' rugged hideout. It was a dark, windowless structure with a damp earthen floor. If nothing else, captivity gave him time to take stock and rest his battered body. He could do it with the calm peculiar to that breed of man who never knew when the sun rose in the morning whether he would live to see it set.

Joshua Dillard was not the kind who

didn't fight to save his skin. Yet nor did he set great store by longevity. His present predicament was far from the first time he'd flirted with death.

He hadn't always taken the chances other men wouldn't. But then the Wilder gang had blown away the light of his life one never-to-be-forgotten day of gunsmoke and blood in San Antonio, Texas, and now his heart would tell him that in going to meet his death he wouldn't be leaving behind much that he valued. Life as he chose to live it these days was a series of adventures, and death in itself would be just another. If Simich had shot him down like a rogue dog, Joshua could have died with a grin on his lips.

His chief regret at this time was that he was being kept from the job he was being paid to do.

Joshua pondered some more before hitting on what he'd try to make his plan of action. He'd play on their fears of imminent exposure and relentless pursuit.

Though they'd tied him, they'd not seen fit

to gag him. Doubtless there was no necessity for it in this out-of-the-way spot. He began to call.

'Simich! D'you hear me? You gotta lemme outa this place!'

He kept up the hollering for several minutes, on and off, before a harsh voice ordered to leave off.

'Shuddup, yuh yowlin' bastard, or one of us ull come in thar an' bust yore jaw!'

'But I wanna talk, damn you! I can't take no more o' being shut up in this airless black hole! Fetch Simich – I got a deal.'

The speaker outside cussed him again, then tramped off.

A short while after he heard booted footsteps returning. Two pairs of them this time.

'What yuh frettin' about, milksop?' demanded Simich.

'He's scairt o' the dark, Butch,' sniggered the man who'd fetched him.

'See here, Simich. I want out of here, an' I'm telling you this range'll be crawling with manhunters less'n I'm let go, y'unnerstand?'

151

Simich hauled open the sagging door on its leather hinges. 'Yuh're in no place to threaten us, stranger,' he jeered. But his eyes were narrowed suspiciously.

'Ain't no threat, mister. I have to report in regular to my bosses by coded message,' Joshua lied. 'If the right words don't get sent by telegraph from Hellyer's Creek real soon, thar'll be big trouble around here.'

The man with Simich growled. 'Why, you sneakin' sonofabitch–!'

Simich restrained him. 'Hold it, Gus. Let 'im lay it out. What's this message gotta say, Dillard? We can't let yuh go, yuh know that.'

'Okay, but I get claustrophobia, you heard o' that? You lemme out o' this place an' I'll write the message down. You can send it yourselves, I guess.'

Simich scratched the side of his big nose, turning the proposition over. He decided to humour his prisoner. He'd no intention of ever letting him go, but if there was anything in this tale of checking in by wire, the details might give him a better idea of who Dillard was with and how he and his cohorts stood.

The outlaw boss nodded curtly. 'Cut his han's free, Gus, an' go rustle up a pencil an' paper.'

Gus produced a vicious-looking Bowie knife with a fourteen-inch blade and sliced through the leather securing Joshua's wrists, before clumping off.

'Don't let 'im try anythin', boss,' he warned over his shoulder.

'Yuh know me, Gus,' Simich said, drawing and cocking his long-barrelled six-gun. 'Any tricks an' I'll blow a hole clean through the bastard!'

Gus returned with a stub of pencil Joshua recognised as being from the contents of his pillaged saddlebags. The paper was the blank side of a yellowing page torn from a mail order catalogue.

'Ain't much light,' Joshua grumbled, flexing his numbed wrists. 'An' a man can't write good pressing on earth.'

Simich's thin lips curled. 'Reck'n our guest kin walk across to the Waldorf Astoria,

Gus. Let 'im use his legs.' He gestured with the Colt. 'But one false step an' it's inta a suicide's grave, Dillard.'

They went to the main cabin where Joshua was shoved before a none-too-clean pine table, its top warped and split. A kerosene lamp swung above it. Flies fed on crusty food stains stuck to the scarred timber.

A buzz of interest from the other occupants marked their entry.

'Git writin', range dick!' Simich ordered. Despite his withering scorn, he was burning with curiosity and leaned forward to watch as Joshua began to put words on the paper. The black muzzle of the menacing Colt wavered away from Joshua's midriff.

Gus, too, crowded up to Joshua, his eyes on the paper.

Joshua moved as fast as a striking rattler. He took one step back and seizing Simich and Gus by the scruffs of their necks smashed their heads together.

Simich's Colt boomed, but his eyes were glazed and the six-shooter went spinning from his nerveless grasp.

Across the room, an owlhoot screamed in mortal terror as he copped the flying lead.

It was all the chance Joshua needed. Dropping to the dirty floor, he scooped up Simich's gun and in one rolling movement shot out the light.

The lamp crashed onto the table in a litter of bent metal and glass, a spreading pool of oil and a flickering wick. Then all at once there was a whoosh and the tabletop was engulfed in a flash of flame.

Clem could think of no way of summoning Dorothy-May back to Hellyer's Creek other than by a telegram to the Pennydale Ford way station. Carefully worded, such a wire should not arouse suspicions at the office in town, as might a cry to farther quarters for assistance against stated or unstated villainy.

The telegraph operator who accepted his message raised an eyebrow and smirked. Clem reddened and was sorely tempted to challenge him to put up his fists. But he knew the man could hardly be blamed, for he'd deliberately couched his summons in ambiguous terms any contemporary might have considered scandalously bold in sentiment and familiarity.

How else could he secure the girl's attention without spilling the beans?

'MY DEAR MISS PENNYDALE,'he had written. 'YOUR EVERY WORD HAS PROVEN SO RIGHT WITH REGARD TO OUR SMALL DIFFERENCES. I LONG TO SEE YOU AGAIN URGENTLY SO THAT I MAY PAY PROPER RESPECTS TO YOU AND EXPRESS MY ADMIRATION. COME QUICKLY TONIGHT FOR WE HAVE MUCH TO SAY AND DO. MY AFFLICTION IS A RAMPAGING LION. YOUR HUMBLE SERVANT CLEMENT P. CONWAY.'

'You sure that "affliction" is right, sir? Don't you mean – ahem – "affection"?'

'No!' Clem jerked out. 'Please transmit the words I've written, operator.'

The telegraph man's tutting was lost in the

ticking of his instrument's needle. He wrote down the incoming message, translating the dots and dashes into words.

While the clicking went on, he thought about his new Easterner client. The poor fish was obviously sweet on – no, besotted with – that harum-scarum way station girl who dressed in men's clothes.

'She ain't the best-looker around, but she sure must have somethin',' he told himself. 'An' by the Lord, this city feller has to be a mighty fast worker with the women!'

Shaking his head, he tapped out Clem's message on the apparatus' key.

Clem returned to the hotel. The lobby was empty; the clerk's desk unattended, presumably for the night, though a bell sat prominently on its empty mahogany top. After waiting by the window in his room for an hour, the anxious New Yorker returned to the deserted lobby and sat on the edge of a horsehair sofa. He watched the entrance expectantly.

Would Dorothy-May understand? She'd

seemed smart enough, and was obviously a good and intelligent reader. After all, she read his novels, didn't she?

Dorothy-May burst upon the scene like a thunder-roll on a summer's night. The pounding hoofs of the black pony that seemed to match her own stormy disposition clopped to a stop by the hitching rail before the hotel steps, and the girl swung down and strode into the lobby with the swagger of a cowpuncher on payday.

Clem jumped to his feet.

'What is this, Mr Conway-Ironhorn?' she demanded before he could open his mouth. She flapped under his nose a crumpled sheet of paper roughly ripped from a telegram pad.

'Thank God you've come, Miss Penny-dale. The message has served its purpose–' Clem coughed – 'though it might not be exactly what it appears.'

'Yuh're damned tootin' it ain't! I never did git writ no love letters nohow, an' us Westerners shore as all git-out don't like t' be joshed by no city slickers!'

'There's an explanation–'

'Reck'n thar has t' be, pen-pusher. Weren't no other reason a well brung-up young lady goes a-ridin' inta town at the drop of a hat. Give!'

Clem wasted no time in outlining what he'd overheard outside the marshal's office. Swallowing his pride, he finished by admitting he'd been mistaken about Virgil Lyons.

Dorothy-May could see in the blinking eyes behind the steel-rimmed spectacles that the revelation had knocked the tenderfoot hard. His book learning was no defence against the hard blows of disillusioning reality. He was staggered that he'd been wrong and she'd been right.

'By crackity, I knew it!' she said, trying hard not to crow. 'The ol' geezer is as crooked as a bob-wire spike. It's jest like I says – he's in Sanders' pocket. An' since Hell'er's Crik pinned its star on Lyons, the hills hereabouts has bin fillin' up with a passel o' godawful, mean-eyed drifters, I tell yuh.'

'But what can we do, Miss Pennydale? Frankly, I'm at a loss. I had hoped that man Dillard would arrive here, but it seems he's still off catching the road agents.' Clem shivered. 'Maybe they've caught *him*.'

'Lawd ferbid! Dillard's our only chance – yuh right thar, Ironhorn. Yore bracin' a gang o' bank robbers with yore Navy Colt w'd be like a rabbit pickin' a fight with a pack o' coyotes.'

Clem winced at her relentless honesty. Dorothy-May didn't spare her words.

'I'm sure Dillard is some sort of range detective. Probably he's working for Wells Fargo. We just have to find him.'

'Wal, I hate bein' a quitter, an' I ain't fer tossin' in our hand, but I can't do nothin' thetaways nohow,' Dorothy-May mused, scratching her red moptop. 'Dillard c'd be up in the hills anyplace from here to Tucson.'

'Maybe he's slipped into town unnoticed,' Clem suggested, not very hopefully. 'We could check round the boarding houses and so on as a last try.'

Dorothy-May regarded him with a degree of pity, but said, 'Bully fer you, Ironhorn! There oughta be some way outa this. We jest gotta find it – an' before t'morrer!'

They trudged out into the street where they considered splitting up and going separate ways to complete the chore faster. The plan was ruled out when it became obvious Clem's knowledge of the town was too limited to conduct his half of the search.

'It's not that I want to drag you into a load of trouble...' Clem faltered, fearing some apology was in order.

'Fer God's sake, I'm awful glad yuh did. I allus did wanna settle th' hash o' that cuss of a marshal. Lion o' the Law!' she scoffed. 'I never did believe none o' them cock an' bull tales. An' as fer thet slimy Sanders, I turned over stones an' seen worthier critters.'

Clem was heartened to have an ally. Clearly the situation was not one in which a gentleman would normally choose to impli- cate a girl – even one who affected mannish clothes and salty language. But her brutal honesty and her steadfastness were characteristics with which he found himself unexpectedly comfortable.

Men were bunched on the walk outside the Silver Buckle as they approached the gaudy frontage of the saloon. They were about to pass them when suddenly Clem clamped a hand on Dorothy-May's wrist and drew her back into a shadowed doorway. He felt her pulse flicker and jump against the tips of his clutching fingers.

Needles of excitement pricked Clem.

The girl stared at him with her big green eyes wide. 'Hey, mister, I thought yuh was all right–' She broke off, realising that he'd no dishonourable designs in pulling her into the darkness. And maybe, to her astonishment, even feeling a pang of regret.

No, Clem's gaze was fixed on the men outside the saloon.

'We haven't found Dillard,' he hissed. 'But I think I've seen something that could lead us to him!'

11

'You'd Better Pray!'

Joshua Dillard wasted no time. The fire was a lucky break. If he could get out of the cabin and to a horse before his enemies could regroup, he'd be away and free.

The flickering light showed him three or four owlhoots still on their feet, and in a quandary. They could block his path and shoot it out with him; they could fight the blaze; or they could save their own skins and flee before the leaping flames took hold and engulfed the place and everyone stupid or luckless enough to be left in it.

Joshua backed away from the men to an open window, covering them all the while with Simich's Colt.

The minute he turned to slide over the sill,

he saw one fellow level a gun on him through the billowing black smoke. Though his eyes were smarting and the dense fumes racked his body with choking coughs, he took quick aim.

His right hand kicked twice as he thumbed the hammer.

It was not the best or surest of shots, but it cut the other gunman down with a stifled sob of agony.

Joshua went through the window.

His last glimpse was of the fallen man crawling frantically along the far wall, one crippled leg dragging behind. And of Gus, back on his feet, hauling Simich out by the boots.

Joshua's mouth set in a grim line and his eyes gleamed like agates. Simich was going to be sore as a smoked badger!

More owlhoots were rushing about outside in the darkness, and horses in the corral, startled by the outbreak of fire, were whinnying and galloping to and fro.

Shouts of alarm rang out as the main

cabin erupted in an explosive burst of smoke, sparks and shooting flame, like a dry bundle of rotten kindling wood.

One last escaper staggered miraculously out of the inferno. He was screaming and his clothing was afire from collar to boots. Joshua thought it might be the man he'd hit in the leg. He fell to hands and knees in the dirt yard between the pens outside. Terrible animal sounds gurgled from his throat as he floundered toward a wooden horse trough. Even his hair was beginning to singe.

Joshua, though hardened to violent death, was sickened. He hefted the Colt, debating whether to end the owlhoot's misery quickly. But the range was at the limit for a handgun, and to fire might draw pursuit.

Joshua ran farther up the slope and thrust into the tall brush at the edge of the timber rimming the hideout hollow. Outlaws were already fanning out, guns drawn, looking for him.

'This way!' he bawled in a guttural voice. 'The bastard's gone inta th' trees!' Keeping his head down and his shoulders stooped, he pointed ahead into the darkness, then loosed off a shot in the same direction.

The ruse worked. With Simich still out of the fray, the irate searchers didn't question the order. They pounded up the slope in full cry.

'Say, Ironhorn, I'd be powerful obliged if'n yuh'd leggo m' wrist an' put me wise t' what's a-goin' on in thet weird brainbox o' yore'n.'

Dorothy-May's peevish whisper had Clem releasing her from his grasp like a guilty boy caught with his fingers round a cookie jar.

'Oh! Y-yes, of course. Pardon me,' Clem stammered. 'A little carried away. You see, unless there's another exactly like it, that man with his back to us over there has Mr Dillard's gun!'

'Wha-at! Which one?'

Clem pointed out Lafe Teed. 'The scruffy, unwashed lout leaning against the rail outside the saloon.'

'How d'yuh savvy it's Dillard's shooter?'

'Well, if it isn't, it's a hell of a lot like it – a .45 Colt Peacemaker with a black grip and a deep crack in it! I swear it's the very same Dillard showed to me on the stage road.'

Dorothy-May wrinkled her freckled nose. 'Looks a kinda ugly varmint. Reck'n we should sail up an' ask 'im where he got it?'

'Absolutely not!' Clem rapped, horrified that his audacious companion might do just that and seizing her wrist again.

'Hold yore hosses, Ironhorn! I was just bein' sassy. I ain't an idjut yet.'

Clem grinned sourly at himself for having taken her seriously. 'Of course not,' he remarked more composedly. 'My mind was occupied by the importance of the discovery.'

'Shucks, if this feller's got a hold of Dillard's gun, he's like t' know what's become o' Dillard!'

'Exactly. I suggest that when he leaves we follow in his tracks surreptitiously.' Clem paused doubtfully. 'That is, if we can...'

'Waal, I dunno about yore surrep – whatever yuh said – but fancy, bookprint words ain't the only thing eyes kin read, Ironhorn. I kin read sign like a 'Pache.'

'You'll do that for me?' Clem asked eagerly.

'Shore I will. Thar's this bank game on an' it sounds a dandy. If we find Dillard, we kin mebbe bust it up – an' Lyons, Sanders an' their whole blasted crowd'll git their comeuppance!'

'Funny how a stroke of luck like this should turn up,' Clem observed. His spirits had been lifted by the chance for action where none had seemed possible.

Dorothy-May's returning smile was restrained by her streak of hard-headed practicality. As she saw it, the opposition still held most of the aces.

'Not so funny, I reck'n, an' we'll judge the luck if'n it works out!'

The outlaws began beating into the brush with a series of cusses and shouts. Joshua saw the flicker of a sulphur match as they tried to pick out the crushed and broken foliage that showed his path.

'He's gotta be around here someplace. He ain't had time t' get fur.'

A swift confab took place in low voices. Then they split up and spread in a creeping cordon, moving toward the forest.

Joshua lay flattened to the ground amongst the scented mesquite that masked a rocky cleft. He scarcely dared breathe and he gripped the butt of the Colt, ready to fire in an instant. An owlhoot passed him less than twelve paces away.

He thought the danger of discovery was gone when the man suddenly halted and looked over his shoulder, eyes suspicious. Almost silently, the searcher padded back toward the covering screen of brush.

Joshua peered between the prickly branches, weighing his chances. The surest way to deal with this would be with a chunk of lead between the hombre's eyes. But using the .45 that way would be sure betrayal of his whereabouts and bring the whole pack of them baying for his blood. So he reversed the big gun in his hands, grasping it by the long barrel.

He let the man take one more hesitant step before leaping up from the ground, Colt swinging.

The iron hit the surprised man with a solid thunk on the side of the head and he collapsed immediately with no more than a gasping grunt.

Joshua sank back beside him into the deeper shadows and paused, tensed for reaction from his victim's comrades. But there was only a murmur of departing voices and the occasional crunch of a boot amongst fallen twigs and dead undergrowth.

Inspired by the success of his action, Joshua swiftly ghosted downslope, heading for the pen where the outlaws' horses were corralled.

He vaulted the five-pole gate and caught hold of the first horse he saw and hauled it by the mane to the fence where riding tackle had been draped untidily by its owners. He got a bridle on the nervous animal with little trouble. The only saddle blanket he could find was a disgusting length of tasseled fabric, the once-soft wool frayed and stinking and matted with grime. But he threw it over, then flung up the best of the saddles and cinched it down.

Intent on preparing the mount as well as he could, and his ears filled with the alarmingly loud snorts of the horse and the chink of the bit-pieces in its square yellow teeth, he didn't realise there was another man among the horses in the corral until he'd swung aboard.

Lafe Teed lunged out of the darkness and grabbed the horse's bridle. In his fist he held cocked Joshua Dillard's own Peacemaker.

'Thet's fur 'nuff, Dillard! Yuh ain't goin' nowhere. Git down!'

Joshua instantly kicked out and lashed at Teed's face with the ends of his reins. They caught the outlaw with flesh-cutting force and blood oozed along the stripes.

A bullet zipped past Joshua's ear. The horse reared.

But it was neither of these things that unseated Joshua and brought him with a bone-jarring thump to the ground.

From his other side, another shadowy figure had leaped like a mountain lion, wild-eyed and snarling. It was Butch Simich who seized his leg and jerked his boot from the stirrup with wrenching force.

Simich had a livid bruise over his right eye where Joshua had slammed his head against Gus'. Now he'd recovered consciousness, he was fighting mad. He kicked Joshua force-fully in the ribs, spitting obscenities.

'Shall I plug 'im, boss?' asked Lafe Teed. 'I jest got back fr'm the Crik an' was wond'rin' what the hell was goin' on when he showed up bold as brass an' helped hisself t' th' grey an' a saddle.'

'Naw!' snarled Simich. 'Shootin's too good fer the smart sonofabitch. He's gonna suffer an' die real slow.'

Alerted by Lafe's gunshot, the rest of

Simich's bunch were straggling back from their fruitless search.

'Truss 'im up an' blindfold 'im this time!' Simich commanded.

Menaced by Lafe with his own gun, Joshua was held strongly to the ground. His wrists were jerked behind him and pinioned, his ankles lashed together. A blindfold was wrapped round his eyes, cutting tightly between his brows and cheekbones.

At Simich's orders he was then heaved across the back of the horse he'd saddled.

'Yuh messed with the wrong man when yuh took on me, Dillard,' Simich jeered. 'But now I've got yuh licked, yuh hear? By the time yuh peg out, by God, yuh'll wish yuh never stuck yore bill in!'

He turned to the gang. 'Saddle up, boys, an' let's ride!'

Joshua felt his horse being led off. Eventually, he sensed he was part of a bunch of riders, heading farther and higher into the hills. Occasionally, thorny foliage scratched his face where it seemed the trail narrowed.

Dust, stirred by the hoofs, filled his nostrils and was gritty between his parched lips.

He heard Lafe involved in long and absorbing conversation with Simich. Excitement ringed their voices. Joshua could only make out snatches of the discussion but certain key words gave him to understand that a plan to rob a bank was afoot.

Joshua was hazy about the time, but after a jogged journey of half an hour or more, the party came to a stop. He was pulled off the horse and dumped on the ground. Simich instructed someone to cut the ropes at his ankles and he was pulled to his unsteady feet.

Simich closed up behind him.

'Now yuh gonna l'arn what it's like to be in a *real* hole, Dillard,' he grated with what sounded like satisfaction. 'Yuh'd better start prayin' them buddies yuh reck'n t' have find yuh purty fast. 'Cos we're lightin' out, an' this here's one hole yuh'll never git out of on yore ownsome!'

Joshua felt a sudden, vicious shove in the

middle of his back and stumbled forward blindly.

Then his right foot went down on nothing but air and he was falling headlong into emptiness. His mouth opened in an involuntary yell that was whipped away as he uttered it.

The plunge could not have lasted more than seconds, but it seemed like several terrifying, heart-lurching minutes. What kind of precipice had he been thrown off? What would he land on or in? Would he lose consciousness before the fall was over, or after?

He struck the bottom of the pit with an impact that forced the last of the breath out of his lungs and sent pain searing up his spine.

Though half-dazed, he was aware of the owlhoots' guffaws and jeers.

'Kin yuh hear me, Dillard?' Simich cried.

Joshua moaned, and it was pretence in only small part.

'Yuh in yore grave, range dick! It was a

shaft sunk by a prospector lookin' for gold lode. But the vein had pinched out on 'im. A mighty sad sorta place, thet hole... So long, busybody!'

The ugly laughter drifted away. And Joshua was alone, facing a very problematical future.

12

Secret Listener

The pain in Joshua Dillard's back gradually subsided and he got back his breath. As best as he was able with his hands roped behind his back, he checked that no bones were broken. He felt more numb with the horror of his situation than with any injury he might have sustained.

The depth of the shaft he'd been pushed down he could only guess at. Prospectors' pits were common in this country, some of them going down a score of feet or more.

A long-gone gold hunter, panning in a watercourse for dust deposits, would have grown tired and impatient at his chore. Then he would have tested his luck at digging, searching upstream for the mineral lode from which the placer values had been eroded.

Using a primitive, self-operated windlass, he'd pick out his 'glory hole' till he could get no deeper, or he was lured by some more promising site. Then he'd move on, customarily leaving the pit as nothing more than a monument to his folly.

Joshua lurched to his feet. His priority was to remove the blindfold so that he might know the worst extent of his predicament. Feeling with his shoulder, he located a jagged outcrop in the uneven wall of the shaft that was at a convenient height.

Then he began the laborious task of grinding away at the piece of cloth tightly wrapped around his head and over his eyes.

He cursed as the rough-edged rock scored the skin stretched tightly over his temple and his face became sticky with the oozing blood.

Blind! In more ways than one he'd lost sight of where he was at. And what.

Maybe, like the canny old marshal, he

should have let the outlaw band fade away untraced into the vastness of this wild country. Their cold-bloodedly murderous raid on the stagecoach had brought them nothing in terms of loot and had therefore been a failure. He'd done his bit and saved the lives of the passengers. But he hadn't been content with that.

The devils that drove him had him forsaking the job he was being paid to do and chasing after the owlhoot killers, with only vengeance on his mind. It was the skeleton in his closet raising its head again. But it was a beautiful head. His memory still clothed it with glowing flesh and filled the eye sockets with bright orbs of blue; crowned it with spun-gold hair.

His wife! Gone, gone, yet always with him, possessing him. Motivating him. But turning him unprotestingly into an emotional cripple. Undermining good sense.

It was his obsession. Hunt the lawbreakers. Bring them to book. *Kill* them.

The tears of his futility further dampened

the blood-soaked rag clinging round his head. But at last the tatters fell away and the cool air wafted soothingly over the hot torn skin.

Night had fallen long since. He had light of sorts though. The moon hung directly overhead, a near-complete disc, casting white light like a big mirror. It was as bad as he'd thought. The stark sides of the prospector's pit were near vertical. It was about fifteen feet to the rim.

No way would he climb out of here without aid, even when he'd managed to sever the cords round his wrists and body.

The saloon girl Cora was licking her wounds in the pokey upstairs room she inhabited at the Silver Buckle.

Her eyes smouldered with anger. Not only was she wild about the alleycat treatment she'd endured from Lucia Marques; she was mad with Dice Sanders. Taking one look at her scratched and battered condition, he'd complained she wasn't fit for work and banished her to her coop of a room. He'd also told the barkeep he was docking her pay. Just as though it were all her own personal fault.

It was little consolation to Cora that Sanders had borne as many scars as herself.

Grinding her teeth with rage, she went to the loose floorboard beneath which she hid a private emergency fund. The small reserve, cached in a muslin tobacco sack, was income from private services to patrons. Cora was good at her job. She'd found customers would often pay extra to the house charges for her very personal touch. Those extra dollars she hadn't felt it necessary to disclose to her employer, but had prudently hidden away.

She prised the board up with the end of a comb, then paused as the sound of voices came clearly to her. Her room was immediately above Sanders' office behind the saloon and she'd often overheard interesting conversations before. But none had ever been as illuminating as the one she eavesdropped on now.

Sanders' voice she'd expected. The other she also recognised instantly. It was the nasal whine of Willie Fulcher, Hellyer's Creek's rat-faced banker. Fulcher was a regular punter at the saloon's gambling tables. He treated Cora with open contempt but she knew that Rose, one of the other girls, visited Fulcher's home regularly. In Cora's opinion the practices to which Fulcher's tastes reportedly ran were unnatural and perverted.

'You're in the red for more than I can continue to carry, Willie,' Cora heard Sanders say.

'It's just a bad patch, Dice,' Fulcher whined back. 'My luck will change, won't it? That's the law of averages. When it does, I'll settle up the IOUs right off, even before I put back the bank money I've borrowed.'

Sanders grunted as though he had doubts. 'The Silver Buckle can't wait any longer, Willie. Mebbe I should drop a line to Wells Fargo. I understand you're going into some kinda joint venture…'

'No, no! You mustn't do that.'

Sanders hardened his voice. 'But I will, Willie, I will – unless you want to join me and certain good friends in a little proposition I've got.'

'I can't sit by and let you destroy my career.' Fulcher was almost pleading.

'So glad you're agreeable, Willie.' Sanders laughed contemptuously. 'I hardly think you'll need your wretched career if you throw in with us on this one.'

'How do you mean, Dice?' The banker's voice became suddenly shrill with anxious suspicion.

'Just that as from tomorrow your bank is knocked over, finished, but your IOUs will be taken care of and likewise your passage out of the territory.'

'I knew it – you're asking me to help rob the bank of the fifty thousand!' Fulcher's reedy little voice rose to a croak. 'Give me a drink, Dice. I've got to think about this.'

Cora heard a bottle set on a table, a chink

of glasses.

'Sure you can have a drink, Willie. But you're in no position to make any other demands. Understand this – we've got you pinched in like a corn in a tight shoe! Now listen good...'

Cora gulped. She put her bleach-blonde head well down and bent her ear to the gap in the floorboards. By the time the pair had done talking, her shapely legs were numb from the kneeling, but she knew it was time she quit Hellyer's Creek.

Sanders was running out on his wife and the town he ran and bled. Nor did it sound like she, Cora, had any part of the future he planned for himself. 'This here is all penny ante stuff,' he'd boasted to Fulcher. 'I could stay in Hellyer's Creek a year more and not make the *dinero* I can collect tomorrow.'

Marshal Virgil Lyons was in the game, too. He and Fulcher would ostensibly be taken off as 'hostages' by a gang of bank robbers. Sanders would ride out on a strong horse, stood by at the livery barn, readied and provisioned for a long haul.

Cora, like others, knew Lyons was wholly Sanders' man. She understood the old marshal stayed in office only by Sanders' sufferance.

She bent her calculating mind to her own situation.

With Dice vanished, presumably Lucia Marques would reign as queen of the Silver Buckle. That would not bode well for Cora. How she hated the woman, flaunting her foreign airs and graces while she had to slave, peddling her sex for measly dollars!

Creek folk admired Lucia; she would probably receive their sympathy. All Cora would get – and had ever got – would be sneers and pity. Any protection or influence she'd had as Sanders' plaything would be gone.

But Cora had no intention of being forced to grovel to Lucia, or worse. Nor did she think Lucia would be content with her lot, humiliatingly deserted in what she'd always patently regarded as the back of beyond.

She spent a great part of what was left of

the night composing a letter. It was a feat that didn't come easy to a girl of little formal education and a hand not much practiced in writing. But the results were to exceed even her hopeful expectations, though that was something she was never to know.

Next morning, just about sun-up, Cora went to the stage depot with her one packed bag and caught the first coach out.

Clem and Dorothy-May had similarly been early risers that morning. The way station girl, true to her word, was an excellent tracker. Lafe Teed's sign was fresh and clear to her keen eye. Clem, surprisingly, demonstrated that he was an adequate rider.

'By crackity, Ironhorn, we're doin' well. I'd had it in mind m' work was gonna be cut out t' stop yuh from a-fallin' off,' she said.

'You chose me an excellent mount to hire at the livery barn,' he returned in exchange for her admiration.

The sun was still in the eastern sky when they reined in cautiously on the timbered ridge above the hollow that contained the deserted line camp latterly used by the Butch Simich gang.

The fire-blackened wreck of the main cabin still smouldered.

'Blast it all!' said Dorothy-May. 'Looks like whosoever was here has cut an' run. Where kin thet blessed Dillard hombre be?'

'And why did that hardcase have his gun?'

'We've had good luck so fur, but now I reck'n we're in fer a spot o' the other kind,' Dorothy-May opined solemnly.

They cast around looking for fresh sign. The girl frowned at the evidence of the much trampled bush where the gang had searched for Dillard.

While they were making their investigations, Dorothy-May's black pony let out a shrill whinny which was answered with a nicker from the cover of the trees.

They recognised Joshua Dillard's chestnut mare the instant they found it, left on dropped reins. Though this was promising, the absence of the owner and his bedroll and saddlebags seemed ominous.

'The damn' murderers have no doubt robbed and killed him,' Clem said.

Dorothy-May nodded. 'It would of bin the smart thing for 'em t' do if'n they got the chance. But we've come too fur t' give up less we *knows* it, I says. An' we'll need Dillard t' go up ag'inst Sanders an' Lyons.'

All this took time Clem knew they could scarcely afford. In the hot ashes of the cabin, they found to their discouragement the unidentifiable remains of a body. Another burnt body had been hastily hidden under rocks behind the shacks. It was not Dillard. Finally, after the inspection was done, Dorothy-May decided the crew that had used the line camp – the stage raiders? – had headed out in one large party father into the hills.

It was hard going, in unmapped country criss-crossed by eroded washes and canyons, but they guided their horses in the steps of those who'd recently gone before.

'Thar's nothin' out this aways 'cept some old mine workin's,' Dorothy-May puzzled.

The rough trail crossed a patch softened by a spring. Here Dorothy-May studied the give-away marks embedded in the dirt and confirmed what she'd been suspecting. The party of riders had passed *both* ways. They'd been someplace, then returned.

'They musta took care o' some business an' then come back straightways...' she pondered aloud.

She thought hard a bit. The repose this brought to her usually animated face gave Clem pause to reflect that she was a most singular person. She had character and a resolute persistence not at once apparent, but infinitely more important to a man than any superficial perfection of profile or complexion. While her courage was in no doubt at all.

'I figger thar was a skirmish at th' camp first off, prob'ly triggered by Dillard,' she said. 'But he was outnumbered, killed mebbe, an' they brought him out here t' dump 'im.'

'Miss Pennydale, you're a wonder! And I think you're absolutely right. I only hope you're wrong about Dillard being killed though.'

'Waal, we ain't seen no outlaws. If they're the Simich mob what's in with ol' Lyons, they've like as not slipped past us on a fork trail, headin' for the Crik. So let's try some hollerin'.'

Dorothy-May cupped both hands around her mouth and filled her lungs. *'Mr Dillard! Mr Dillard!'*

The yell echoed and re-echoed through the gaps and over the rocky ridges.

To their excitement, a faint cry answered the call.

'Here! Over here!'

'Mr Dillard!' Clem shouted back. 'Mr Dillard, where are you?'

'In a prospector's pit, damnit!' Joshua's amazed voice floated back.

Clem and Dorothy-May homed in on his frantic call and peered down the hole.

'Mr Dillard! Lordsakes, are yuh all right?' the girl asked anxiously.

'I'm cold, hungry an' weary. An' madder

than a trapped grizzly. But I ain't got no broken bones. During the night I figgered you folks an' Mrs Sanders would be my only hope, though you've turned up a damnsight sooner than I'd dared expect.'

A lariat was fetched from Dorothy-May's saddle and Joshua thankfully hauled himself out of the sheer-sided hole.

Then Clem explained what had brought them so promptly, and the trouble that was brewing fast, even now, in Hellyer's Creek.

He pulled a watch from his vest pocket. 'The bank opens at ten, I understand. That means this Simich gang could strike as soon as they hit town.'

Joshua didn't feel up to a hard, fast ride. But he had a score to settle with Butch Simich, who had now added to his sins by leaving him to die a slow and agonising death.

'Let's go,' he said.

And after they'd recovered his chestnut, Clem and Dorothy-May had trouble matching his pace on the trail to Hellyer's Creek.

13

Dillard Goes to the Bank

Lucia Marques found Cora's letter shoved under the front door. It must have been delivered to the smart Sanders residence behind the Silver Buckle sometime during the night.

The retired actress supposed at first, when she saw it from the head of the stairs, that it had come from her husband. He'd not returned to the house since he'd fled to his saloon after the previous afternoon's bitter confrontation.

She'd spent a sleepless night, turning over all manner of ways in which she could punish him for his disloyal and contemptible treatment of her.

Somehow she would have her revenge,

then she would shake off the toils of this back-country hellpit and leave him to stew. Once the news of his affair and her fight with Cora became town gossip, she knew the humiliation would humble her to the dust. That would be more than she could stand.

She picked up the crumpled envelope and frowned, not recognising the scrawled handwriting.

Two minutes later the mystery was no more.

Lucia was livid. 'He's deserting me, the stinking polecat!' she fumed.

She was devastated anew. Not because she was losing Dice Sanders – and Cora was rubbing her nose in it – but because he was pulling off a coup that would make him free to roam the world while abandoning her in this dump. No doubt he believed that, with no other support, she would be forced to stay, enduring the squalid grind of a rugged frontier town. Such a life sentence of abasement would have to be served, all the more, before knowing eyes that would leer at her smugly from the doltish, bovine faces of the Hellyer's Creek rabble!

Lucia determined that such a living death was not to be. But first she would settle Sanders' hash for good and all.

She dressed quickly and flinging a shawl over her shoulders left the house on an urgent mission.

Willie Fulcher's bank was unarguably the most solid structure in Hellyer's Creek. Much of it was built from the stone that had been blasted and hacked out of the rock on which it stood to create a secure and fireproof vault.

It was here, Dorothy-May said, that the Wells Fargo money would have been taken by the deputies who'd retrieved it from the site of the stagecoach wreck.

Dorothy-May was fortunately a mine of local knowledge.

Joshua Dillard assiduously obtained and absorbed most of this and other information when they broke their journey at Pennydale Ford. Here food and proper drink, though taken on the run, put new life into his bone-weary body.

At the way station he also equipped himself with a disused gun rig belonging to old Ezra. Precious minutes had to be wasted while he cleaned and oiled two Colts – old Model 1860 Army in .44 calibre.

He fastened the belt about his flat hips. 'With luck it mebbe won't come to a shootout, but we gotta be prepared,' he told his two companions.

He knew the odds he was taking on were stacked high against them. If it came to gunplay, he was one professional against a gang of seasoned lead-slingers. He had just these two amateurs he could count on to pitch in when the going got rough.

'We'll try subterfuge in the first instance,' Joshua said, and explained a rudimentary plan.

'I'm counting on two things at the outset,' he finished. 'That Willie Fulcher wouldn't know Butch Simich from Adam, nor the gang him – and that we get in first.'

The *mañana* mentality held sway in Hellyer's Creek during the forenoon, it appeared, much as the siesta did in the afternoon. The drab town was notable for its lethargy. No one took much notice when they rode in, seemingly unhurried, and left their mounts at the livery barn.

There was no sign of Butch Simich or any of his roughneck crew.

But they were alarmed to see a covered wagon had been drawn up alongside the bank. The operation masterminded by Sanders was all set to go, it looked.

'Fade into the woodwork, like I said,' Joshua ordered, 'an' whistle me the signals on cue.'

Joshua crossed the dusty main drag and stepped inside the bank. Blinking to adjust his eyes after coming out of the harsh daylight, he walked over to the teller's wicket.

'I've come to see Mr Fulcher,' he announced quietly.

The bored teller looked him up and down without interest and nodded to a polished oak door bearing the gilt legend 'Private: William S. Fulcher'.

'He's back there in his office, I guess. Try knockin'.'

Joshua went to the door and did so.

A high-pitched, nasal voice bade him enter.

'Mr Fulcher?' Joshua asked, closing the door on his back. He was confronted by a thin, sharp-featured man, whose ashen complexion was mottled by tiny red veins where it stretched over his prominent cheekbones.

The man's eyes darted about their sockets and his fingers fiddled nervously with the leather-bound desk blotter. 'Mr Simich?'

Joshua didn't disabuse him. 'Sure.'

'Wh-where are your men?'

'The boys'll be right along, mister. How about you show me the way into this vault, huh?'

Fulcher nodded and his teeth chattered. 'The day-to-day money we keep in the safe in my cashier's office,' he gabbled. 'But access to the vault is through a trap in the floor right here.'

He rolled back a piece of carpet and produced a bunch of keys, two of which he turned in separate locks set in the floorboards. A section of the flooring lifted on oiled hinges. A stone flag lay a foot or so below the floor. On top of it was an iron pinchbar.

The banker's fear for his safety loosened his tongue and made him anxious to co-operate. 'The stone lifts easily with the bar and gives access to wooden steps into the vault,' he rambled on. 'Once you're down there, it's about as big as this office, though without much headroom, I'm afraid.'

But Joshua was lending him only half an ear to his whine. He knew he didn't have much time – maybe none to wait and glean whatever else Fulcher might volunteer. Swiftly, he stepped up behind the little man, caught him in a strangling neck grip and stuffed a bunched kerchief into his mouth.

He felt the man's Adam's apple bobbing up and down in his scrawny throat.

'Hold still or I'll throttle you,' he growled.

Fulcher complied. Joshua could smell the sweat of his fear as he completed the gag with a ready-knotted bandana that he pulled tight.

With distaste, he divested the startled banker of his coat, vest, shirt, string tie and keys before lashing his wrists and ankles with lengths of cord.

Then he turned his attention to the flagging above the vault. He levered up the stone block and lowered the trussed man down. He quickly followed and manoeuvred the banker's helpless form behind a heap of the canvas moneybags he remembered from the Tucson stage.

Dorothy-May led Clem to the livery barn across from the bank.

'I know Ned the hostler an' thar's a handy loft with a winder over the harness room,' she explained. 'It'll be a cinch t' see every-thin' thet goes on in th' street from up thar.'

Going into the stable, the pair were surprised to pass Lucia Marques coming out. Clem bid her a good morning and was set to inquire whether she had recovered from the previous day's ordeal. But the saloonkeeper's ex-actress wife brushed past, barely acknowledging them.

Clem shrugged and followed Dorothy-May down the stable aisle. A rafter lantern struggled to boost the dim light. Haltered horses stood in stalls on either side.

The hostler Ned was ankle-deep in straw, rubbing down a warm, lathered gelding with a piece of burlap.

'Up in the hayloft?' he asked Dorothy-May curiously, then gave Clem a beady stare. 'Anythin' yuh like, gal, but jest watch yuhself, eh?'

They left him to his work, muttering audibly to himself. 'Ain't nothin' runnin' to pattern no more. Didn't think thet filly messed with the menfolk … an' the Sanders dame agoin' hard ridin' afore brekfus! No accountin' fer nothin', I say.'

Dorothy-May groaned. 'I ain't one to get sore about no gossip, but this c'd plumb ruin a gal's reputation!' she told Clem.

After Joshua had hidden Fulcher in the vault, he returned without delay to the office, shutting the trap and rolling back the carpet. The next part wasn't as easy. When he'd bundled his hat and own comfortable range clothes out of sight under the desk, he discovered the banker's garments wouldn't fit his powerful frame. In the end, he resorted to cutting the side seams of the shirt and vest and the back seam of the coat. The last touch to his flimsy disguise was a broad eyeshade.

As an afterthought he pulled the window blinds, hoping the dimmer light would aid his deception. He'd only just seated himself in Fulcher's big leather swivel chair with a stifled sigh of relief when from the street outside there came a single, high-pitched whistle.

The fake robbery was about to begin.

Heavy footsteps clumped into the outer office and the sounds of altercation broke out. The door swung open.

'I tell you, he already has a visitor!' the teller was protesting.

Butch Simich and Lafe Teed strode in arrogantly, not even masked. They were followed by Gus, who hung behind to stomp on the foot of the pursuing teller and shove a hand over his face, thrusting him to the floor.

'Button yore lip, small fry!' Gus snarled.

Then he came in, kicking the door shut behind him.

'Awright, Fulcher,' said Simich. 'Git th' blasted vault open then play dead, will yuh?'

Joshua gratefully ducked behind the massive desk and rolled back the carpet. Until the stone slab was raised, it would be fatal to his plan if they spotted his split jacket or recognised his face.

He backed off as Teed grabbed the iron bar and levered up the slab.

The outlaws were now confidently ignoring Joshua, clustering round the opening to the vault. It was time to act.

Very slowly, Joshua rose to his feet and took off the eyeshade. Pushing aside the banker's coat he drew both .44s, levelling them at the backs of the group. His thumbs were on the smooth hammers. He cocked the guns with a loud double click the instant he began to speak.

'Freeze, the lot of you!'

'Gawdamighty! It's the bloody range dick – or his ghost!' Teed blurted incredulously.

Gus' hand whipped toward his gun.

Joshua fired without compunction. The shot crashed out, a tongue of flame roared from the muzzle of one Colt – and Gus screamed with the sudden agony of a shattered wrist.

'You can have the same medicine if you want it,' he warned the others. He made a motion with the smoking gun in his right hand. 'Climb down into the vault real snappy, all three of you,' he ordered.

Muttering curses and futile threats, the owlhoots went down the wooden steps. The second the last head went below the floor, Joshua closed in and tipped the poised slab with his foot. It fell with a crash into the aperture.

'Caged, you mangy wolves!' he gritted with satisfaction.

Inside another minute he'd slammed down the trap and locked it.

So far only one shot had been fired, but that was enough to send the affronted teller in the front office scuttling out the building in panic and rushing for the marshal's office.

'Mr Lyons! Mr Lyons!' he hollered, his voice trembling.

All along the street, townsfolk jerked out of their customary apathy came to doorways and peered from windows. A man running and shouting. What the hell was going on?

'A holdup at the bank! A holdup!'

Marshal Virgil Lyons came onto the walk outside his office and met the teller in the shade of the awning.

'What is all this?' he asked importantly, drawing himself up to his full height and throwing out his chest. He knew full well the answer to his question, but he had to play the part assigned him by Dice Sanders.

This was his swan-song in Hellyer's Creek, to his career as a law officer. He was determined it should look good. After today, the Lion of the Law would be no more. He'd be taken 'hostage' by the bank robbers, never to be seen again. In reality, he would retire, south of the Border maybe, with heaps of *dinero* and a whole new identity.

'Three men have busted into Mr Fulcher's office,' the teller panted. 'There was a shot! I think they must be robbing the bank.'

Lyons adjusted his Stetson on his majestic head of white hair. He called to the deputy in his office.

'Hold the fort, Kelly,' he said gruffly. 'I'll jest step along the street an' sort out this foolishness.'

He moved out into the centre of Main

Street and paced slowly toward the bank, savouring his last moments of law-enforcement glory.

As word of the robbery passed from mouth to mouth all around him, the street cleared and Lyons fondly imagined the curious ducking back into cover, watching their town marshal with breathless admiration.

Clem and Dorothy-May watched from their vantage point at the loft window above the livery barn, but their breath was already bated. It had been since they'd heard the shot ring out inside the bank, and seen the panicky teller go running up the street.

Who'd fired at whom? Was Joshua Dillard in control, or had his scheme to thwart the robbery already failed? They'd no way of knowing.

'Thar's nothin' we kin do 'cept keep our eyes skinned an' await developments,' Dorothy-May summed it up.

'I believe there are more of those owlhoots hidden down there in the wagon,' said Clem anxiously. 'I saw the cover move. And here comes the treacherous marshal, damn his eyes!'

'The ol' faker! Givin' hissel airs like he's stridin' t' some big showdown instead o' jest goin' t' join his crooked pals. Wal, lets hope he gets a big surprise!'

But they cherished no illusions that the battle would be over and won if he did. Put in a corner, Lyons would be a tough nut to crack.

'Get ready to give Mr Dillard the two whistles, Miss Pennydale!' Clem reminded her.

14

The Shootout

Joshua Dillard strained his ears to catch the second of the whistled signals from Dorothy-May above the muffled yelling and cursing going on beneath the floor of Willie Fulcher's office.

Two whistles. That would be notice of Marshal Virgil Lyons heading down the wide, stamped-dirt street for the bank and what he thought would be his getaway and his fortune.

Joshua made a swift decision. He'd have Lyons like a rat in a trap by just staying in the bank. But if the marshal in his desperation tried to turn the tables on him, Joshua would prefer the confrontation out in the open. Where he could unmask the man before witnesses and fair play could be seen to be done.

Therefore, he pulled on his own vest and hat and pushed out into the street, his jaw set grimly and his eyes narrowed against the hot glare of the sun.

Lyons' confident step faltered when he saw Joshua Dillard. His rheumy hazel eyes opened wide with disbelief.

For just a moment the pose had cracked and weakness showed in the marshal's leonine features. Untypically, Joshua felt pity rather than anger. This man was the dupe rather than the villain.

The sympathy died an instant death.

'Dillard!' Lyons roared, his wits seeking a way to retrieve this unexpected turn of events. 'I'm takin' yuh in fer bank robbery!'

'You've got it wrong an' you know it, Lyons,' Joshua countered the accusation. 'Your pards are prisoners in the bank, an' you're washed up, finished. I got witnesses you're in cahoots with the Simich gang.'

Beneath the drooping white moustache,

Lyons' lips twisted in a grimace of frustration and pure hate. His hand shook as he jerked a thumb at the star on his vest.

'Watch yore mouth, Dillard!' he bluffed. 'Yuh're talkin' to the law.'

Joshua shook his head, but kept his unwavering gaze pinned steadily on the marshal's every move.

'You ain't gonna be wearing a star for much longer, Lyons. You'll be facing charges before a federal judge, that's a promise.'

Lyons snarled savagely. 'Mebbeso yuh won't git to actin' on no promises, saddle bum,' he ground out. 'Mebbeso yuh've mouthed off too many *lies* already!'

The marshal's hands hovered at his sides, scant inches from the butts of his shooting irons.

Joshua felt the tension rising to fever-pitch. This was a man whose gun rep was second to none – a town tamer, the legendary nemesis of countless badmen. A man who reckoned his draw was lightning fast. Was he just kidding himself when he said he was as sharp as ever?

'It's no lies I'm talking, Lyons,' he said coldly. 'It's your moment of truth. But if it's threats you're making, mebbe I'd better accommodate you.'

Joshua had said it now. The unspoken challenge was accepted. He stood alone, solid as a rock, his legs braced slightly apart.

Motionless.

A deathly hush had fallen over the street. Every man and woman in the place watched, waited.

Lyons acted. His hands swooped swifter than preying hawks. To most eyes, the movement was no more than a blur culminating in two crashes of gunfire that rang between the false fronts of the clapboard buildings like thunderclaps.

The acrid reek of gunsmoke wafted lazily on the hot air. For interminable seconds, it was as though the world had ended and all was eerily still and deafeningly silent.

Then Lyons' gun dropped from his spasmodically clutching fingers with a thud, kicking up a small cloud of dust at his feet. His knees bent and his eyes glazed and rolled. He collapsed in slow motion into a heap.

Before he died, he made an effort to rise, staring about him in stupid, stunned surprise in his last brief return of consciousness. 'Fastest … gun,' he gasped.

Blood bubbled to his lips and he fell full-length on his face and didn't move again.

Joshua lowered his borrowed Colt .44 feeling as drained as though he'd run a marathon. He'd felt the wind of Lyons' slug, but was unscathed.

It was in that moment of exhaustion and relief that an urgent cry rang out from somewhere over his head.

'Dillard! Look to your back!'

From a box seat as it were, Clem and Dorothy-May watched the drama played out on Main Street with a helpless, heart-thumping fascination.

'Why, the dirty, perjurin' ol' stinker! It's

'nuff t' make yore blood boil,' Dorothy-May said as Lyons attempted to accuse Joshua Dillard of bank robbery.

'My sentiments exactly,' Clem returned crisply.

When the confrontation suddenly blossomed uglily into a gun duel, they were aghast. But Clem retained enough presence of mind to keep his eyes peeled for developments on the wider scene. Consequently, the moment his bespectacled gaze detected more movement in the wagon alongside the bank, he was ready to let rip a cry of warning.

'Dillard! Look to your back!'

Three Simich owlhoots, tiring of waiting for their leader's summons to assist with the transfer of the Wells Fargo coin to the wagon, and now distinctly alarmed by the altercation on Main Street, tumbled from the wagon, six-shooters drawn.

'Blast the range dick down!' one of them raged.

After shouting his warning, Clem had

bounded for the loft's ladder, snatching out his Navy Colt. Dorothy-May stayed at the window, pulling her own gun from the low-slung belt round her slim hips.

Joshua was already whirling and swinging up his drawn Colt to meet the new attack, but the redhead loosed a slug at the leading owlhoot and he dropped his weapon and clutched his shoulder in pained disbelief.

'Ambush!' he screamed, uncertain where the disarming shot had come from.

His partners ducked back behind the wagon.

Joshua dived to the porticoed entrance to the bank, taking cover behind one of the substantial pillars.

Clem joined the fight from the shadowed doorway of the stable.

Instantly, a vicious crossfire was blazing and screaming between the three points.

A slug ricocheted explosively off the stonework by Joshua's head. Dust spurted into his eyes, temporarily blinding him, and his cheek was cut.

It was at this crucial moment that a heavy figure in a rusty-black broadcloth suitcoat over a flashy brocade vest boldly slipped behind him and into the bank.

Dice Sanders sucked greedily on the smoke from a fat Havana cigar, letting it escape slowly. He'd spent the night on the couch in the backroom behind his office at the Silver Buckle. His fleshy body was still sore and bruised from the drubbing dealt him by his termagant wife and he'd not slept well.

Hence his special appreciation of the first cigar of the day. That and the comfort of knowing that before the new day was out he'd be richer by ten thousand dollars – his personal share of the Wells Fargo loot. Such money could buy him more than eight hundred acres of prime land. It topped what a well-paid working man could expect to earn in ten years.

Sure, he'd be on the dodge. But that had happened many times before in the ex-gambler's life and the *dinero* could buy all kinds of protection and open up unheard-of routes to distant paradises.

He'd no regrets at quitting his saloon and rackets in Hellyer's Creek. They were small-time stuff, and once Lucia Marques started yapping he would become a figure of derision anyway, which would undermine his power in this broken-down burg.

His day-dream was broken by a tentative knock at the door.

'Mr Sanders sir, are you there? Mr Sanders?'

It was his half-wit of a head barkeeper.

'Of course I'm here, fool,' he growled. 'What is it?'

'It's Cora, Mr Sanders.'

Sanders didn't want to be reminded of the busty wench whose attractions, by his twisted reckoning, had pitched him into crisis and necessitated the radical rethinking of his future plans.

Females! They were nothing but a trouble and a curse with their wheedling ways and their vicious little tempers. Forever honey-talking and taking, then changing their minds and digging in the claws.

'The hell with Cora! Tell the little whore she can clear off. Ain't no man gonna look at her while she looks like she's been in a cat fight.'

'She has, Mr Sanders.'

'She has what, damnit?'

'Cleared off. Her room's empty an' her bag's gone.'

Sanders' mouth tightened and his piggy eyes grew black. He suspected the barkeep was enjoying needling him.

'Well, clear off yourself an' leave me alone, willya?' he roared. 'I got other fish to fry!'

For all he cared, every rat could desert the sinking ship. His own arrangements were already made and a readied and provisioned horse should even now be stood by for him at the livery barn. He still owned the god-damned tumbledown dump, and this last convenience was the grand total of its worth to him.

Sanders sloshed some of his best whiskey

into a chunky glass and, feeling a little calmer, settled down to wait.

Two and a half hours later, the first shot reawoke his irritation.

An odd outbreak of gunfire was not of any particular note in Hellyer's Creek, which attracted the human flotsam run out of more settled communities, but Sanders was on edge.

'Damnation! Sounds like from the bank. There ain't meant to be shooting,' he muttered.

He decided he'd go take a look-see. Outside, the saloon had already emptied and up and down the walks, the word was already buzzing around that the bank was being held up and that Marshal Lyons had been summoned.

Sanders hadn't wanted the robbery to become a circus. 'Curse that Simich!' he grumbled to himself. 'Ain't no need for this stuff. Fulcher and Lyons have orders to go along quietly, an' he's been told that.'

It was Sanders' intention that the money

should be rolling out of town, with the marshal and the banker seemingly the gang's
hostages, before news of the robbery became
widespread.

But when he saw Joshua Dillard step out
of the bank onto Main Street, he knew that
things had gone terribly wrong.

'Who the hell's this sonofabitch?'

Teed had told Lyons that the agent who'd
queered the stagecoach attack had been
taken prisoner and Teed had gone back to
the outlaw camp with instructions that in-
cluded his prompt dispatch. Yet here was
someone going up against Lyons.

Was this the interfering Dillard, who was
supposed to have been taken care of once
and for all?

And where was Simich and his crew?

From that point on, Sanders dazedly saw
the situation rapidly deteriorate for him,
with his cats-paw marshal beaten to the
draw in a duel Hellyer's Creek hadn't seen
the likes of in a patriarch's age.

Then the owlhoots from the wagon made

their play and there was pandemonium.

Women screamed and bystanders scattered. And hot lead flew in all directions at once.

Sanders swore explosively. 'This is damned crazy!'

His second plan had miscarried.

Fifty thousand dollars had been theirs for the taking in Fulcher's vault. Now it seemed to be slipping from their certain grasp in some insane foul-up.

Sanders chewed on the frayed cigar in one corner of his moist lips and grunted determinedly.

'Naw! I ain't quitting town without some of that blasted loot – not on anyone's sweet life!'

Drawing an ivory-handled revolver from a shoulder holster, he flitted along the boardwalk toward the bank on feet surprisingly light for one of his fleshy bulk.

For once, he was going to have to take care of his own dirty business.

An owlhoot slug screamed deafeningly off

the pillar by the bank entrance, throwing stinging splinters and dust into the eyes of the skilled gunfighter who crouched there.

The man, whom Sanders perceived was his number one enemy, was temporarily blinded.

Sanders made his dash.

15

The Aftershocks

Sanders darted straight across the empty chamber known grandly as the banking hall and into Fulcher's private office.

'Where in damnation have you gotten to, Fulcher?' he bellowed, seeing nothing but another unoccupied room.

It was then he realised the muffled yelling and cursing he heard was not part of the general din from outside, but was coming from under his feet.

'Hell fire! They're locked in the vault.'

He didn't try to look for keys. He smashed the timber around the locks with repeated shots from his revolver that almost split his eardrums in the closed space.

Simich was hopping mad and blundered

up into the room like a crazed steer, his bellowed invective filthy.

'We bin twisted, yuh great slug! Thet badge-totin' bum Lyons let Dillard get inta th' place, the useless slob!'

He neglected to acknowledge, even to himself, that his incarceration of Dillard alive in a supposed grave, had been a prior failure.

Sanders' shifty eye strayed to the shaded window which he knew gave on the side alley and the waiting wagon.

'Don't lead off at me, brother,' he told Simich. 'The polecat that did it's out front. Your other men have got him pinned down.'

'Let's get 'im, boys!' Simich bayed, and stormed out with his two partners at his heels.

Sanders smirked to himself, then hurried down the steps into their former prison. He despised such hell-raising riff-raff, and had previously left their handling to Lyons.

But they had their uses and he'd every hope they'd create the deadly diversion he needed.

This time it was Dorothy-May, left by herself in the hayloft perch, who saw what was going on behind Joshua Dillard's back.

'Judas priest! Thet four-flushin' brothel-keeper has ducked into th' bank.'

She clattered down the ladder to join Clem in the livery barn doorway. 'We gotta git Mr Dillard away from thar afore Simich an' his pack come out a-roarin',' she said.

'Just so, Miss Pennydale, but he's trapped there by the men behind the wagon,' Clem replied bitterly. 'It looks like the ruffians will win the day yet!'

Dorothy-May tossed her red head defiantly, her chin set. 'Never say die, Ironhorn! They don't in yore books!'

'This is not a book, Miss Pennydale,' Clem explained patiently.

But the girl wasn't listening. She made a sudden leap and snatched the unlit pitch pine torch from the metal bracket by the stable door. Without pause she struck a lucifer on the seat of her pants and set the torch afire. All her stringy might then went into hurling the flaming brand at the wagon.

In seconds the dry, sun-baked canvas was going up in a gusty roar. The wagon was swept from end to end by the fierce blaze. The owlhoots behind it broke cover and ran for their lives.

Joshua Dillard, his eyes cleared of dust, lost no time in leaving his cramped position in the bank doorway and giving chase.

Clem downed one of the fleeing trio with his Navy Colt. Joshua took another, and the third threw up his hands in surrender.

'Leave 'im t' me!' Dorothy-May cried, running up and flourishing her gun. 'Sanders is bustin' Simich an' his pards outa th' bank!'

Joshua got back in front of the bank entrance in time to hear the stomping of angry feet inside. Simich and the two others charged out into the daylight and were temporarily dazzled.

Joshua promptly stitched the dirt at their feet with a line of heavy .44 slugs.

'I'm right in front of you, scum, an' the

next ones will be a lot higher. Drop the guns an' get your hands in the air!'

They let their guns go. They hoisted their hands slowly, grudgingly. 'Yuh got the drop on us, I guess, Dillard,' Simich admitted harshly.

With the back of his free hand, Joshua wiped the blood from his cut cheek. His arms felt heavy, like he had lead weights attached to his wrists. His chest was heaving as he slowly regained his breath.

But that was the end of the shootout at Hellyer's Creek.

It wasn't the end of the action. After Simich and his men had been locked up in the town jail, Joshua returned with Clem and Dorothy-May to the bank.

Joshua looked broodingly at the smashed window in Willie Fulcher's office. 'That's the way Sanders went, while we were rounding up the owlhoots.'

'He's suttinly skeedaddled. Ned the hostler says he had a bronc all saddled up an' waitin' at th' livery barn,' Dorothy-May said. 'I c'd kick m'self fer not thinkin' o' thet.'

'You've done magnificently, Miss Pennydale,' Clem objected to her self-criticism. 'And you certainly mustn't blame yourself for anything. Why, we all owe you our lives!'

'I'll get the louse yet,' Joshua promised. 'Ned had careful orders not to feed Polly too much grain, an' though she ain't properly rested, I aim to get on Sanders' trail straightaways.'

Joshua was as good as his word. But Dice Sanders had a fresh horse and he'd quickly left the stage road and headed into the hills, where the terrain was rough and boulder-strewn and the going hard.

The one bonus was that the little-travelled trails meant that Sanders' sign was not confused with others'.

Night closed in and the moon rose, bleaching the country with a ghostly radiance.

'He ain't stoppin', ol' hoss,' Joshua murmured. 'So I guess we keep plodding on the same.'

He hunched himself in the saddle and pushed on with a dogged persistence, though his body ached for rest after the rigours of the previous night and day.

Joshua also had a fear that in his exhausted state he would nod off and amble into a trap. He didn't underestimate Sanders' cunning. If the man was counting on pursuit, he'd never find a more isolated place in which to make moves to eliminate it.

Up in these hills, it would be easy to pick off a rider and hide his body.

Toward sunup, when a band of sky in the east had already began to lighten to grey, Joshua figured from the fresh marks tramped in the packed dust that his quarry had slackened pace and was making frequent stops, dismounting and leaving the trail more often than any fit man should need to.

Joshua yawned and stretched and his saddle trappings creaked as he eased his seat on the leather. In straightening up, his gaze scanned the country ahead – and was drawn to the boulder-shot yucca-grown draw that looked to be the beginning of a canyon.

For a moment he thought he saw a flicker of light there, such as might be made by a dying fire. He sniffed. Was there woodsmoke on the air as well as the scent of sage?

Because the immediate footing was flint-hard granite that didn't take a hoofprint, and Sanders' passing was therefore unclear, he decided to pull off the narrow trail and investigate.

Maybe Sanders had pitched a late camp to snatch a few hours' rest before daybreak.

And sure enough, this quickly looked to be the case.

Joshua left his horse ground-tied and crept up on the site, slipping quietly into the scrub at the canyon entrance. He grinned to himself when he heard what sounded like a man groaning.

He's snoring or he's injured himself, he thought.

Joshua wriggled the last few yards Indian-fashion, using his elbows to drag himself noiselessly over the sandy soil. He looked down into a small hollow at the back of the canyon.

Sanders' horse moved about restlessly, as though sensing something amiss. The fire was burned out, just a heap of smouldering charcoal, that looked to have never been much in the first place.

Sanders was prostrate beside the heap, his face the colour of its palest grey ashes. The other notable things were that his tailored broadcloth pants were grossly soiled and a smell of sickness hung on the air.

And he mumbled deliriously. He talked about running all his life, toward something or away from something. But running. And for what? To die in the dust with his guts drained dry, his body an empty husk...

Joshua rose to his feet, confident of no threat to himself from this pitiful wreck who so few hours before had been the boss of Hellyer's Creek.

'God!' he breathed, revolted by what he saw.

Sanders heard the exclamation and turned

his little eyes, now fever-bright, upon this new torment. He gave a dry-retching cough, clutching his lower body.

'Poisoned!' he gasped. 'I'm done for, mister. Too weak to move. Do your worst, sod you!'

He groped for a leather canteen on the ground beside him, and spilled the last of its contents. Whether his action was deliberate or accidental, Joshua had no means of telling. The spillage – the splatters and globules – was rapidly sucked into the dust till it was no more than a dark stain.

'Some two-timing bastard–!' Sanders began again.

'Who?' Joshua asked. 'Who did it, Sanders?'

But the stricken man may not have known. He did no more than mumble incoherently before passing out.

Joshua waited only till the sun rose. By then Sanders was dead and had not spoken again.

The weary trail rider made no attempt to

bury the body. He didn't even so much as touch it. In the purple haze overhead, the buzzards wheeled, celebrating his departure with their evil calls.

When Joshua was gone, they swooped lower and in circles that became ever smaller, till their stark, sinister shadows loomed large, passing over the waiting feast.

First one, then another, flopped warily onto the ground. Their macabre cackle filled the echoing canyon like a witches' incantation. They jostled for position around the vile repast.

Hooked beaks busily tore flesh from bone.

'Mr Dillard's back.'

Dorothy-May told the news to Clem Conway breathlessly, having hurried to the Hellyer's Creek hotel ahead of him from the Pennydale Ford way station.

Clem was more than pleased to see the vivacious redhead again. In truth, he hadn't stopped thinking about her all day, musing and wondering... He thought he might be more than half in love.

And he was all fired up to spring a new hero on the literary scene. Marshal Virgil Lyons, the Lion of the Law, might be found to have the proverbial feet of clay. But it no longer mattered a whit.

Clem was already drafting in his stimulated imagination the opening chapters of a new epic of adventure – *Daring Dot, the Heroine from Hellyer's Creek*. He was convinced it would be his most enthralling and successful work to date.

His rival purveyors of blood-and-thunder were in for a real shock. 'Move over, Edward L. Wheeler!' he'd exulted when the inspiration had struck. 'Clement P. Conway, alias Nate Ironhorn, is set to take the New York publishing scene by storm!'

But here was the real Dorothy-May, bringing word from the detective fellow Joshua Dillard of the final outcome of the shootout and the fate of the man whose dastardly scheming had sparked it.

'Poisoned!' he exclaimed. 'Well, there's a

turn-up! Who did it?'

The question was still being asked next morning when the pair met again, along with Joshua, in the hotel's lounge.

Another sensation had also arisen. Lucia Marques had hired a spring buggy and ridden out of town not to be seen since.

It was inevitable that this new mystery, and that of Dice Sanders' poisoning, should be linked.

'She was at the livery barn before the shootout. We saw her,' Clem remembered.

Joshua said, 'Ned has admitted she might easily have tampered with Sanders' warbag, which was packed and waiting in the harness room. Then there was the unusual business of her ride that morning. Apparently someone saw her out by the Mexes' sod house.'

'The cholera!' Dorothy-May cried, her green eyes wide with horror.

Joshua nodded gravely. 'Looked a damned sight like it. Mebbe Lucia Marques had had her fill of Sanders' infidelities. Mebbe she got wind of his tricky plan to run out on her with all o' that money.'

'But at least it's ended badly only for those who deserved it,' Clem said. 'Your Wells Fargo chiefs should be well-pleased with your efforts, Mr Dillard.'

'Wells Fargo chiefs? Me?' said Joshua.

'Of course! You were shadowing the stage-coach to keep an eye on the special consign-ment. And just as well, seeing that fool banker Willie Fulcher blabbed about it to Dice Sanders.'

'Now wait a minute, feller! That's a misconception. I ain't never worked for no Wells Fargo.'

'Then what–? Who–?' It was Clem's turn to look baffled. He blinked behind his steel-rimmed spectacles and his brow furrowed.

'I'm a freelance agent,' Joshua explained. 'A soldier of fortune of sorts. My gun is for hire when the *dinero* is right and the job takes my fancy.'

'Wal, spit it out, Mr Dillard,' Dorothy-May demanded bluntly. 'Ain't no call t' keep yore comrades-in-arms in th' dark. Who was yuh actin' fer?'

Joshua sighed. 'I guess I'll have to come clean. I was commissioned as an undercover bodyguard for Mr Conway by his New York publisher. Seems the gent had awful nightmares about losing his top writer on a damn' fool jaunt into this here lawless West.'

'Good God!' said Clem.

'Huh!' said Dorothy-May. 'An' all th' time I thought it was me a-lookin' after the poor lamb!'

'Never mind. Now he's survived the outlaw lead, mebbe you can take care of his *social* life.'

'What! Me?' Dorothy-May squawked. 'I ain't got no time fer parties an' dancin' an' frilly frocks!' But Joshua thought he heard an embarrassed note in her voice and the truth was, she was already dreaming of a wedding, maybe next Spring…

As for Joshua Dillard himself, he was thinking he'd have to resign his commission and settle for the measly hundred dollars advance on account of his expenses.

He could save Clement P. Conway from the hardcases, but he was damned if he could rescue him from the toils of a designing woman.

Aw, well, maybe Wells Fargo would make him an *ex gratia* payment.

That was something for him to dream about as he rode on out of Hellyer's Creek.

The publishers hope that this book has given you enjoyable reading. Large Print Books are especially designed to be as easy to see and hold as possible. If you wish a complete list of our books please ask at your local library or write directly to:

Dales Large Print Books
Magna House, Long Preston,
Skipton, North Yorkshire.
BD23 4ND